TRULY ENOUGH

By the Author

Truly Wanted

Truly Enough

Visit us at www.boldstrokesbooks.com

TRULY ENOUGH

by

J.J. Hale

2023

ISBN 13: 978-1-63679-442-6

THIS TRADE PAPERBACK ORIGINAL IS PUBLISHED BY
BOLD STROKES BOOKS, INC.
P.O. BOX 249
VALLEY FALLS, NY 12185

FIRST EDITION: JUNE 2023

CREDITS
EDITOR: JENNY HARMON
PRODUCTION DESIGN: STACIA SEAMAN
COVER DESIGN BY TAMMY SEIDICK

Acknowledgments

Thanks to everyone I already thanked in Book #1. You're all still awesome humans who enable me to write books about queer, neurodivergent women kissing a lot, and that's pretty cool. Also a big thank you to Lego for providing me with ample procrastination methods. Lastly, thank you to anyone who took a chance on a new author and picked up my first novel. I've always said that if my writing made even one person feel a little more understood, it would be worth it. The words of encouragement from people who took time out of their days to tell me they enjoyed my story, or to tell me it made them laugh or cry or lose sleep just to finish it (the highest compliment!) have been the best way to motivate my brain to keep writing.

To my nan, who Lexi gets her middle name from.
You always believed I could do anything I put my mind to,
even when putting my mind to anything felt impossible.
I wish you could be here to see my dream come true,
but I'm very glad I don't have to try to hide the sex scenes.

CHAPTER ONE

Robyn Moore got home from her day shift as a firefighter and took in the chaotic scene, in what was supposed to be her living room, with a sigh. Several half-painted canvases were strewn across the oak coffee table they had recently found at a car boot sale and spent a weekend upcycling. Paint pots dotted between them precariously, threatening to interfere with the pattern on their newly revived table. Finally, her eyes landed on her haggard-looking roommate as she sat on their old leather couch, staring straight ahead, paintbrush in hand. Her face was creased in what appeared to be more anguish than concentration.

"Earth to Lexi, what's going on here?"

She waited a moment for Lexi to hear her words, something she'd gotten used to in the three and a half years they'd lived together. A beat later, her friend snapped out of it and lifted her honey brown eyes to meet Robyn's. They'd been roommates long enough that Robyn knew when not to break Lexi's creative flow, but what she'd witnessed when she walked through the door had been anything but flowing.

"Shit, sorry, time got away from me. I'll clean this place up."

Lexi gathered her stuff together as she continued to speak. "The four walls of my bedroom were providing no inspiration, and with the studio closed, I just brought my supplies out here for a little while."

Lexi finally took a breath and stopped the frantic tidying, confusion furrowing her brow. "I meant to have this tidied before you got back. Did you finish early? What time is it?"

Robyn furrowed her eyebrows and cocked her head to the side. "It's seven p.m., Lex. I left for my shift at eight a.m., and you were getting set up in your room…"

Lexi grabbed her phone and checked the time as if she needed to see it with her own eyes. "Where the hell did the day go?" She slumped into the chair and let her head fall against her hands. "I need to get this piece done and it's just not happening."

Robyn made her way around the mess toward her friend and placed a comforting hand on her shoulder. "What you need to do is eat, because I'm damn near certain you haven't done that yet today."

"But—"

"But nothing." Robyn cut off the protest that followed. "You tidy this up. I'm ordering food. Then we're going to relax and watch serial killers get what's coming to them. Okay?"

"Serial killers and relaxing probably shouldn't go hand in hand, but surprisingly they do. Thanks, Robbie."

Robyn brought up the app for their favourite fast-food place and clicked repeat order. It was a Tuesday night so they wouldn't be waiting too long. She gathered utensils along with the necessary crime binge-watching supplies—chocolate and sugar-loaded sweets. Lexi had the place mostly cleared by the time the hot food was in Robyn's hands, and she made her way to their worn-in and far too comfortable couch.

"When the delivery guy starts asking how my shift was, it probably means we need to cut back on ordering from this place, right?"

Lexi stared into space, neglecting to respond. Robyn realized that Lexi was still caught up in her own thoughts. She waited a moment for Lexi's attention to return to her before speaking again.

"What's going on, Lex? I can hear your thoughts from here." Robyn started to dole out the food, giving Lexi the time she needed to vocalise what was causing her distracted demeanour. Robyn was used to Lexi taking a few moments to become present, but tonight she seemed more distant than usual and maybe even sad.

Lexi laid her head against the back of the couch. Her warm ivory skin and ash blond hair were pale against the contrasting colour of the dark leather. Given her own jet-black hair and brown eyes, Robyn often joked that Lexi was the sunshine to her darkness. She had nicknamed her Sunny not long after Lexi moved in. The nickname first made an appearance mostly accompanied by sarcasm or scowls, but it had softened over time. It was as close to a term of endearment as Robyn got.

As Robyn looked around the apartment, she noted, not for the first time, that their contrasts went beyond just physical appearance. The darker colours Robyn was naturally drawn to accentuated the bright display of decor Lexi adored. But over the past couple of weeks, the darkness in the background seemed to have descended upon Lexi.

"I just don't know what to do, Robbie. I feel like somebody came in and sucked the passion right out of me and I'm left with this." Lexi gestured toward the still near blank canvas propped up on the art easel in the corner. "It's not fun anymore. And before you say it, I know I'm an adult and life isn't all fun. I need to pay rent, bills, and buy too much take-out food. But if I don't meet this next deadline, I won't be able to afford any of those things. Never mind ruining the reputation I'm trying to build. But I'm stuck."

Robyn turned fully now and sat cross-legged, plate in her lap as she pointed her fork, prompting Lexi to start eating. "I wouldn't say that. Just because you're an adult doesn't mean you need to hate what you do. I've seen how much you love doing this. So, what changed?"

Lexi chewed, her forehead creasing as the silence enveloped them. Eventually, she shrugged. "That's what I've been trying to figure out."

Robyn hated seeing her usually cheerful friend so lost. It brought forth the fixer in her, the person who wanted to solve all the problems of the world, especially for the people who meant the most to her. Which was a short list. If only she could get a better glimpse into the brilliant, creative brain she admired so much and see what was causing this block.

Robyn wasn't the artistic type. Her strengths lay far more in the physical realm. The closest she ever got to creativity was the occasional decorating project Lexi dragged her into, in which she mostly did the parts that involved taking things apart and putting them back together again. She didn't know art, but she knew Lexi. She had heard about people getting blocked, losing their muse, whatever you wanted to call it. But in the years they'd lived together, Robyn had never witnessed it happen to Lexi. Usually, the struggle was getting her roommate to stop painting, not to start.

They ate in relative silence after that, both lost in their thoughts until their plates were clear. Robyn took them and placed them on the coffee table, now free of the earlier chaos. She reached an arm out and Lexi moved beneath it, lying her head against Robyn. It had taken a long time for them to get comfortable, or rather for Robyn to get comfortable enough to be physically close to one another like this.

Physical closeness was something Robyn usually kept separate from emotional closeness in her relationships.

Her family wasn't the hugging type, and any other physical affection she sought was usually a one night only thing. Emotions just complicated that. But somehow, Lexi made it easy, almost natural, to be close. It had happened so slowly Robyn didn't even remember when it changed.

Robyn grabbed the remote and turned on the crime show they had been bingeing recently on the evenings they were both at home together. They stayed that way, huddled together, watching the drama unfold before them. Robyn pondered how she had ended up spending her off-shift evenings curled up on the couch, holding her roommate. More importantly, how in the world it had gotten to feel this comfortable. She was providing support to a friend in need, one of her favourite people in the world, that was all. That had to be all.

Because she was not about to be a walking lesbian cliché, dreaming about the impossible and wasting time pining for her straight-as-hell roommate.

❖

The next morning, Lexi Lynch walked the short distance to the studio space she rented at the local theatre. Despite the exorbitant rising rent costs, she loved living in the city and being able to walk or grab a bus to most of the places she needed to go. She had no half-completed pieces to transport from her apartment, considering yesterday had been a total disaster. The time had slowed down and then sped up all at once until she was left staring at an empty canvas with a chest full of fear. Today could not be another failure.

She walked in the side door of the theatre, waving at the front-of-house staff she'd grown to know well, before making her way into her studio room at the back. It was small, but it suited her. Too much space led to too much distraction, and right now she needed to focus and get the pieces she had already committed to finished. She could feel the tension headache start behind her eyebrows as she stood before another blank canvas, willing the creative buzz she knew so intimately to come and engulf her.

Minutes turned to hours, her headache increasing, while the only buzz around was the overhead light, too loud and too bright. The paintbrush hadn't even dipped into the paint today. Her already low spirits sank to the ground, and she bit her lip to keep the tears from falling. Her phone rang, and it snapped her out of the dark downward spiral of her thoughts. She stared at the name lighting her screen and clicked to answer.

"Hey, Lexi Lou." Her father's nickname for her, spoken in his familiar sing-song voice, enveloped her. "How's my favourite daughter?"

She smiled despite herself and wiped a stray tear from the corner of her eye. "That doesn't work when I'm your only daughter, Dad."

He chuckled lightly as she got up, gathering her stuff together as he replied, "Still true. Are you ever gracing us with your presence again, sweetheart?"

The teasing in his voice was evident, but Lexi could tell he was concerned. It had only been a couple of weeks since she had last seen him, but since she often visited several times a week, it might as well have been a year. She paused, trying to decide the best course of action. Being in the comfort of her childhood home, eating a proper home-cooked meal as her parents fussed over her, was exactly what she needed right now. But it would mean conversation about the career he had never approved of in the first place. A career that was currently at a standstill, maybe about to head down a steep decline.

Her father meant well, but he had never been good at hiding his fear about the instability of Lexi pursuing art full time. The thinly veiled questions disguised as curiosity were easier to manage when she had positive news to convey. But she had never been great at hiding anything from her parents either, and it wouldn't take long for him to realize things weren't so rosy with her job right now.

Despite that, the grumbling of her long-neglected stomach answered for her. "I'll be there soon, old man." She laughed at the string of good-natured epithets that left his mouth at her jibe. She hung up and headed out the door toward the bus, leaving the canvas behind her, still as blank as when the day had begun.

❖

With a satisfied stomach and a comforted heart, Lexi made her way to her apartment that evening, feeling lighter than when she had left it that morning. As luck would have it, her father had steered clear of any questioning about her career this time. Lexi had an inkling that luck had little to do with it, from the looks her stepmom, Simone, threw at her father anytime the conversation even hinted in that direction.

Simone had been in her life almost as long as she could remember, so the *step* part was mostly unused. She was Lexi's mom in every sense that mattered, including the fierce protectiveness she displayed, and her innate sense of knowing when something was up with Lexi, even if it went unspoken. They were worlds apart in physical appearance, with Simone's rich umber skin and salt-and-pepper hair, but their deeper connection and understanding of each other couldn't have been closer with genetics.

Her father had done his best in stepping up as a sole parent when Valerie, the woman who gave birth to Lexi, had walked out on them. Lexi would forever be grateful to Simone for coming into their world and allowing her father to go from survival mode to the full, beautiful life they had created as a family. Meeting Valerie for the first time three years ago only solidified to Lexi what she'd always known. She had one mom, and Simone was the reason Lexi was able to pursue her dreams in the first place.

Lexi set her bag down beside the door and padded across the apartment to the room on the right, from which her cosy pyjamas were calling her. She changed into her soft yellow pjs, dotted with bunnies, that her nephew had gifted her for her birthday, complete with bunny-shaped slippers. She smiled as she slid them onto her feet and headed back out in search of a nice cup of tea to end the day.

Robyn's bedroom door opened, and a tall, beautiful woman stepped out, closing the door behind her. The woman stopped and waved a quick hello, her long blond curls somehow looking perfect, even after she had most likely just rolled out of bed. Lexi was all too aware of her own current attire as she took in the woman's strapless dress and killer heels. Lexi awkwardly waved back a beat too late, as the woman made her way toward their apartment door. She couldn't remember if she'd ever seen this person before, but it was hard to keep up with the revolving door of Robyn's bedroom.

An irrational zap of jealousy shot through her. It had been so long since she'd been with anyone, that honestly, she'd stopped thinking about it. Painting had taken up most of her time both in life and in her brain as she had established herself the past few years. Dating had not just taken a back seat but had fully left the vehicle.

Yet recently, when women left Robyn's room, or on the nights Robyn never made it home at all, an ache would take up residence in her chest for a while and refuse to budge. Maybe dating wasn't completely off her list of priorities after all. Maybe this ache was nudging her toward finding someone to feel close to, even if it were only for a night.

Her only frame of reference for that type of closeness was one steady boyfriend, who had been her best friend for years and whom she trusted completely before they took the next step in their relationship. The relationship had ended amicably, passion never having played a huge part. She had yet to understand that longing described so often in the media. That lust at first sight, all-consuming pull to another person. She could tell when people were aesthetically pleasing to her, sure, but she didn't have the time to invest in falling for someone. Without an emotional bond, the attraction never sparked. One-night stands had never been her thing, which is what led to this long, self-inflicted celibacy. Maybe now she was ready to try.

Robyn came out of the room just then, and Lexi focused her attention back to the task at hand as she put the kettle on to boil.

"Did you have a good evening?" Robyn enquired as she grabbed a cup to place next to Lexi's before adding a tea bag.

"Not as good as yours, it seems." Lexi's mumbled reply was out before she had a chance to consider the words. As she realized what she said, she shot her head up to take in Robyn's slightly amused expression.

"I just mean…well…she had very long legs."

Robyn sputtered a laugh as Lexi's cheeks heated.

"So, Freya having long legs equals a better night than yours? Good to know your type."

Robyn shot her a wink before she turned to make them both tea, and Lexi took a moment to gather herself from the unexpected interaction. Robyn turned to hand Lexi the cup.

Her deep brown eyes held a hint of something Lexi

couldn't quite place. As Robyn ran her fingers through her dark hair, Lexi paused with her hand wrapped around the mug, waiting for the words that seemed to hang between them.

"Well, I hope your evening was good all the same. Night, Sunny."

Lexi retreated to her room as Robyn headed to her own. She sat in the safety of her bed with her steaming cup, still aware of the unease in her chest. Up until recently, she had never worried about losing out on anything, or anyone, by focusing all her attention on painting. But she was beginning to think that maybe it couldn't fulfil everything she needed or wanted. The passion missing from her art left a noticeable absence in her life. An absence she was suddenly longing to fill.

CHAPTER TWO

"Moore, I need to see you in my office." Robyn jumped at her Station Officer's words, doing what was asked of her immediately. She rarely set foot in his office, but there was one place in her life she was happy to follow orders, and that was right here in the station that had become more home to her than anywhere else.

"Yes, sir?"

Officer Milton had been running the station for far longer than Robyn had been a firefighter. He was direct and a little standoffish, but always fair and protective of his team. Still, it was a little like getting called to the principal's office in school. She had far too much experience with that, and no good memories. Her nerves appreciated that, as usual, he cut straight to the point.

"There's a sub-officer position coming up soon. You've been a firefighter long enough to apply, and I'm happy to support that application. So, get it on my desk sooner rather than later and I'll process it from there."

Robyn was taken aback. Obviously, the sub-officer rank was the next step for her, but she hadn't considered it happening anytime soon. She was still a relative newbie to the service. Her years on the job paled in comparison to most of the crew, bar the couple she had trained with.

"Is that an issue, Moore?"

Robyn realised she hadn't replied when Officer Milton spoke again. "N-no. No issue, sir. I'm just surprised I'm next in line." She was honest about her hesitance. The last thing she wanted was bad blood with her team if they accused her of jumping the line. They relied on each other in life-or-death situations, and she couldn't afford to feel anything but comfortable around them.

Officer Milton sat and looked at her, then nodded to the seat across from him, which she slid into. "I'll be frank with you, Moore. You've worked here long enough to know the members of this shift are excellent firefighters, but they are not leaders. They come in, do their jobs, and leave at the end of shift to go home, satisfied at having done an important day's work. But you strike me as someone who wants more. You're a leader, which you've shown from the start. Is any of that incorrect?"

Robyn's chest tightened and her heart warmed at the words. It may not have been an emotional speech, but it was the highest compliment she'd ever heard Officer Milton give. "No, sir. This station, this job, this is my home. I want to do whatever I can to be a part of continuing its success."

Officer Milton nodded, and she could have sworn there was a hint of a smile, but it was gone before she was sure. "Good. Applications are in the usual place, have it to me by the end of next shift."

At that, Robyn was dismissed. She got up, nodded, and walked out the door, feeling both elated and terrified. Being a firefighter meant being in dangerous situations daily, yet somehow the thought of filling out a form scared her more. This is what she had worked so hard for. This is why she'd spent hours training and learning everything she could about not only her job but every rank above her, while her colleagues slept or chilled out in their downtime.

This next step was what she needed to start making the changes she knew would benefit them all. The ideas bubbled inside her as she made her way to the filing cabinet to grab the application and then headed to the cafeteria. She grabbed a sandwich from the counter and sat at the table with the application in front of her, studying the questions she'd already read many times before.

How would her father feel if he were here to see her now—would he be proud? She smiled, knowing the answer already. Memories surfaced of seeing him in this exact station, the pride on his face as he told her about his promotion. She was too young to understand what it meant, only that her father was like a superhero in his suit. Everyone she met that day talked about the amazing things her father did, all the people he saved. They all looked up to him, and she was no different. To this day, his name shone bright on the plaque in the officers' area. She'd lost count of the number of times she traced the letters of his name, Declan Moore.

"Sub-officer? You sure you wanna go down that route, Red?"

Robyn turned her head as Tommy Brennan, her colleague and closest friend in the station, slid into the seat beside her. The nickname Red had stuck from their first day of training together after she had initially shot down his initial suggestion of Birdie. That one was never getting a response from her.

"Yeah, Brenn, some people around here don't want to sit on our asses all day watching game shows."

Tommy would take the jibe as intended, even if it would sound harsh to anyone outside of their tight-knit crew. This is what they did. They ran into burning buildings, or dealt with the horrors caused by cars, and risked their lives for others. In between that, they made fun of each other and found humour everywhere they could. Tommy was her brother, and that came with all the fun of sibling banter.

"More fool you. Hey, I fully support your pursuit of power and control. Don't think I'm ever calling you Officer Moore, though. You'll always be my little Robyn red br—"

"Finish that and my first act as sub-officer will be your firing, Brennan." He laughed just as the alarm went off and they sprang to action, the application form abandoned as the job she loved called her. She suited up and jumped into the engine as Tommy took the wheel.

As much as he joked, he loved this job just the same as she did. His promotion to driver not long ago had him on a high all week, but she knew he didn't have his sights set on officer. Managing a team wasn't his strong suit, and he was comfortable admitting that. She admired him—what you saw was always what you got.

Some days Robyn didn't know who she was or what she wanted. Her focus had always been her career, and it looked like she was about to head in exactly the right direction for that, even sooner than she had planned for. The loss of her father and witnessing her mother's grief had her sworn off love and relationships since she was a teenager. In her head, love equalled pain. So, she was happy to risk her life for other people daily, but risking that kind of heartbreak was outside of her comfort zone.

Her thoughts briefly floated to Lexi's sparkling eyes and her smile that lately were dimmer than usual. Lexi's sadness was taking up more of her brain space than she was willing to admit even to herself. It was something Robyn couldn't stop wanting to fix. But as the adrenaline pumped through her veins and they hopped out of the truck, her thoughts of Lexi faded, and nothing but the job mattered.

❖

Lexi sat across from her sister Sam as they sipped tea and caught up on the past few weeks. It was still surreal to Lexi that not too long ago she hadn't even met Sam. Now she couldn't imagine life without her.

Lexi grew up an only child, despite many years of hassling her parents for a sibling. So, a few years ago when her father revealed she had a sister, Lexi was a mixture of excited and angry. Her relationship with her father had always been good, though a little strained due to his lack of support for her career choice. The few months following the revelation had been rocky.

She resented him for not telling her sooner that her birth mother had another child. A sort of grief enveloped her, for all the things she'd missed, the what-could-have-beens. Eventually, she understood, as with everything else in her life, that he was just trying to protect her. As much as it frustrated her, she was thankful for the man that had turned his whole life around so he could raise her and protect her in ways nobody had done for him.

When Lexi found out about Sam, she wanted nothing more than to find her. But with very little information to go off, she figured it would never happen, even in a city as small as theirs. She had no idea if Sam had stayed in the area. Through sheer chance, Sam reached out to her, and Lexi was thankful every day for the series of events that led to the close bond they had shared since.

She focused her attention back on Sam, realising she had

been daydreaming the past few minutes. Sam wouldn't mind. Lexi was grateful that Sam didn't need constant engagement from Lexi when they were together. She was comfortable with silence and shifting focus and appreciated that Lexi was comfortable with the same. They often spent hours in each other's company flexing their creativity in their own ways.

It had started when Sam mentioned to Lexi about body doubling, and how it was a tool used a lot by people with ADHD to focus better. Sam explained that having someone present helped her focus on her own task, even if they weren't working on the same thing. Sam often worked on her website designs while Lexi painted, and Lexi had been happy to help. It wasn't long before Lexi realized how much it helped her too. It was a testament to the relationship they had built and the ease with which they existed together.

"How's the precious cargo my sister-in-law is carrying?" Lexi asked.

"Already ruining my sleep, and the kiddo's not even here yet." Sam exaggerated a yawn and Lexi laughed.

"I don't think you can blame the baby-to-be if your wife is keeping you up late."

"Can too." Sam grumbled, but the smile that accompanied the words told the true story.

Sam had introduced Lexi to her friend Brooke shortly after they met. Sam and Brooke were clearly so far beyond friends that Lexi assumed they were a couple the first time she met Brooke and her adorable son Finley. Sam and Brooke had been a constant support to her since then. She got to be maid of honour at their wedding a year ago and had gained not one but two sisters, along with the cutest nephew. And now another kid to spoil rotten was on the way.

"What about you? Are you going to dip your toes back into the dating pool anytime soon?"

Lexi flashed back to the thoughts she'd been having along similar lines, but she wasn't sure exactly how to convey them. She shrugged, aiming for nonchalant.

"You know how it is. Us artist types aren't cut out for love. I pour all my passion into my creations and, well…nobody wants to play second fiddle to a canvas now, do they? Not that there's much in the way of creations right now."

Lexi aimed for a cheerful tone, but the concerned look on Sam's face meant she missed the mark.

"You mentioned when we were texting you've been struggling with that. No improvements?"

Lexi shook her head at Sam's question and sighed.

"I just can't seem to find that spark again. I've always had too many ideas running around my brain, I usually couldn't keep up with getting them onto a canvas. But they've just stopped."

Sam nodded before asking, "Is there any particular reason you can think of? Did something happen?"

"These commissions. The guidelines I was given for them are very rigid, and the mere thought of it bores me. I can't move past it. Knowing I need to get them done and the looming deadline just sends me to this place where even my own creative ideas can't find me. I'm stuck."

"I completely understand that." Sam's words were a surprise to Lexi.

"You do? You just…always seem so focused when I'm around while you're designing websites. Something that still amazes me as you pull it all together."

Sam smiled and shook her head lightly.

"I've been in that place many times, Lex. I almost lost an important client one time. They were an up-and-coming finance company, and they were paying great money, but I had no interest in what they did. Or in the strict, boring designs they wanted implemented. It took a lot of bribing myself to get through that project."

Lexi laughed, grateful to hear she wasn't alone in this.

"I should just be able to do it, though, right? This is what I want to do with my life. I need to be able to get it done, and I am so frustrated with myself that I can't. I spent hours staring at the canvas the other day and suddenly Robyn came home, and the day was gone, and nothing."

Sam tilted her head, a curious expression on her face.

"You know I have ADHD, right?"

Lexi nodded, a little unsure where this was coming from, but knowing Sam usually had a point behind her segues.

"I'm not sure how much you know about it besides the bits and pieces I've told you."

Guilt slowly crept in as Lexi waited for Sam to continue. She kept meaning to read up about ADHD and learn more for Sam, but she always got overwhelmed when she tried googling it. Especially since most of it was geared toward parents.

"Basically, ADHD is terribly named. It's not a lack of attention. It's more of an abundance of attention. My brain wants to pay attention to so many things that sometimes it means I struggle to pay attention to my work, or any one thing. Regulation is the real issue. There is one thing that counteracts that, though, that's called hyperfocus. Have you heard of it?"

Lexi shook her head, glad that Sam didn't seem bothered by her lack of knowledge.

"It happens with something I really love or am interested in. Usually something I'm very passionate about. I can hyperfocus to the point where time sort of disappears. I could spend hours designing websites and forget to eat or drink or even pee. It seems contradictory to what people assume about ADHD. But it's not always something I can control. If I could, I'd be far richer than I am right now."

Lexi laughed along with Sam, but her brain was whirring. What Sam was describing sounded familiar. She thought back to the many times Robyn would return to the apartment and Lexi would be shocked at the time. Or the years her father spent reminding her to eat between paintings or had to stop her from creating something so she would get some sleep.

"The reason I'm saying this is because it could have something to do with your creativity issues. You mentioned these commissions aren't something you're particularly interested in and suddenly the passion you've had is hard to muster. It could be related. Plus, ADHD can be genetic. Passed from parents to kids. And with Valerie's history, a lot of that may have stemmed from untreated ADHD. Sometimes, knowing there's an underlying reason can help you figure out how to tackle it."

Sam's phone rang right then, and Lexi gestured for her to answer, grateful for the time to process what Sam just implied. Lexi would know if she had ADHD, right? Surely someone would've picked up on that by now. Her parents were caring, attentive, almost too much if you'd have asked her as a teenager.

"Sorry, that was Brooke. Maddie's not doing well since the break-up, so she's taking Finley over there to cheer her up. I promised to arrive with ice-cream later."

A ball formed in Lexi's chest. The break-up. She had completely forgotten about it. Maddie was Brooke's sister-in-law from her first marriage, but they had spent so much time hanging out together at Sam and Brooke's house she felt more like extended family to Lexi. Lexi had been so caught up with this block to her creativity that she hadn't even remembered something as significant as her friend's break-up. She couldn't remember the last time she even asked how Maddie was.

"Shit. I suck. How is she holding up?"

Sam shrugged in reply. "You know how it is. It was a mutual decision. They are still so young and wanted different things from life. He wanted to travel, spend a couple of years working abroad, but Maddie is a homebird. Plus, she just started her new job. It's hard when they still love each other, but she isn't willing to go, and she doesn't want him to stay and resent her. Love is weird, sometimes."

Sam was right about that. There was no villain in this story, no bad guy they could hate on to help their friend through it. The romances on-screen or in books depicted this great, all-consuming love that overshadowed everything in your life. A bond that could only be broken by an earth-shattering dramatic problem that turned love into hate. Apparently, real love meant giving up parts of who you were to become half of a whole with somebody else. Lexi couldn't imagine that ever being the case for her.

She certainly couldn't imagine Maddie ever being anything less than the passionate, vivacious woman that she was. She hoped one day Maddie would find someone who understood she was more than worth staying for, but Lexi couldn't fault someone for wanting to explore the world beyond their small island.

"I get it. You know it was similar with Ethan and me. The wanting different things part, at least. He was ready far too soon for the settling down with a white picket fence and kids part of life, while I was wholly committed to pouring myself into making a career in art happen. I loved him, at least as much as I could. But I loved painting more." Lexi shrugged before continuing, remembering the shame that encompassed her when she first admitted it to herself. How embarrassing it had been to realise she was more fulfilled by putting a paintbrush to a canvas than by her steady, dependable, sweet boyfriend.

"There were only so many times I could see the wounded

look on his face when I blew him off because I got lost in a piece. If I had continued down that path, he would've resented me for leading him on. And honestly, I would have resented him for making me feel guilty about something that, until recently, only filled me with joy."

Sam nodded, her eyes full of understanding.

"And hey, it was for the best. He's happy now, with two little girls and a wife who hangs on his every word. White picket fence and all."

A soft smile brightened Sam's face as Lexi smiled in response.

"Do you think you'll ever want that?"

They had somehow come full circle to Sam's original question, and Lexi took a moment to really consider it this time.

"Honestly, I haven't been attracted to anyone in recent years. I've been too busy building my portfolio and meeting my awesome long-lost sister and creating art. It's strange, I know, but I don't really feel attracted to anyone unless I care about them already. And I haven't given myself much time to form that kind of emotional closeness with someone new."

Sam nodded and smiled softly at Lexi.

"So, you're demisexual? I don't want to assume, so correct me if I'm wrong, it's just what I picked up from what you said."

A lightness surrounded Lexi and she was so grateful to have people in her life who just understood these things without her having to find the energy to explain them. She would never take for granted how different things could be if she didn't have that.

"Yeah, that's the conclusion I came to when I read up about it a while back. I haven't spent much time figuring out what that means for me, but lately I've been thinking maybe I want to. My focus right now, though, needs to be on figuring out how to get these commissions done. My love life will have to wait."

As they stood to leave so Sam could go on her ice-cream hunt, Sam pulled Lexi in for a quick hug.

"Think about what I said. Regardless of the why, maybe you need to figure out what your brain needs right now to make this work instead of just expecting it to work because it has to. And don't put the love life stuff on the back burner for too long. You are an amazing artist, Lex, but you are an even more amazing person. You have more than enough to give to the right person without losing any of that."

CHAPTER THREE

I'm just concerned, you know that. I don't want you wasting your life."

Robyn let out a frustrated sigh and held the phone away from her ear for a minute to avoid blowing up at her mother again. Lexi walked through the door as Robyn paced around their small kitchen area. She took in Lexi's daisy-covered yellow sundress that was so perfectly her. It made her happy, despite her annoyance with the current conversation she was having with her mother. A conversation she had endured too many times.

After a few deep breaths, she replied in the calmest voice she could conjure. "Not being in a relationship isn't wasting my life, Mom. It's not going to be a stain on the family name if I show up to the party solo." She may have let a little whine into her tone on that last bit, but she was only human.

Lexi dropped her bag and grimaced in sympathy as Robyn bit her lip to stop words she would regret from tumbling out. Words like how her mom would be attending solo too, just like she had for the past twenty years. Life had never moved on for Marie Moore after the fire that killed Robyn's father and ended her idyllic childhood as she knew it. Despite that, her mom still expected her to just pair up, marry, and provide her with grandchildren to dote over. As if seeing the shell of a person her mother became when she lost the love of her life hadn't ruined the happily ever after idea in Robyn's mind forever.

Marie hadn't cared that Robyn was gay when she shared the information with her as a rebellious, emotional teenager. The lack of response had disappointed Robyn, who was hoping to get some attention, good or bad. Some sign from her mother that she still cared. But all Marie cared about was that Robyn would settle down with someone, anyone, who would make her life meaningful. As if protecting their community and being a good person wasn't enough. Robyn had long ago realised she would never be truly enough for her mother. She was a living reminder of the man she could never live up to. A man who not only protected their community but raised a family and loved his wife all at the same time. The kind of life he always talked about wanting for his kids too.

Now that both her younger sisters were married with children of their own, Marie reminded Robyn often that she was the only one not fulfilling her father's wishes for them. She might not ever have said it in quite those words, but Robyn always understood the implications. Robyn was letting him down.

She paid little attention to the rest of the call about finalising plans for her sister and brother-in-law's tenth wedding anniversary party. The idea that her little sister was already married ten years was terrifying, but that's what happened when you eloped with your childhood sweetheart while you were both still in college. It's also what happened when you wound up pregnant with said sweetheart's kid, but they didn't talk about that. Plus, Robyn's niece was awesome, so she was partially grateful for her sister and brother-in-law's irresponsibility.

After the call ended, she placed her phone on the counter-top and walked to the couch, flopping down face-first and screaming into one of the many bright cushions Lexi had scattered around.

"You okay there, Robbie?"

Lexi lifted Robyn's legs and slipped under them to sit beside her, placing them back down in her lap. Robyn mumbled unintelligibly, not yet ready to let go of her anger. But if Lexi continued to absentmindedly massage her calves, Robyn couldn't hold on to her anger much longer. She turned onto her back to face Lexi and plopped her legs back where they had been. Her bare skin connected with the top of Lexi's knee as the dress she had admired earlier rode up Lexi's thigh. Robyn sat up straighter and placed her feet on the much safer floor.

"I'm fine. You know how my mom is. If I'm not betrothed between now and my sister's anniversary party next week, I'll have once again broken her heart and brought shame upon the family."

"She realises what year we're in, right?"

Robyn laughed at Lexi's quizzical look and shook her head.

"My mother is still living in the past. Frozen. Probably stuck in a time when life made sense to her and everything wasn't spiralling out of her control. When I think about it that way, I feel bad for her. I just…wish she saw *me* and not the woman she wishes I was."

"I wish that for you too, Robbie." Lexi's voice was softer than before with a hint of concern.

This conversation had gotten too deep too quickly for Robyn's liking. Although Lexi had been her roommate for years now, Robyn wasn't one to spend time discussing her deepest, darkest insecurities or bonding over their shared fears. Robyn rarely shared a lot of personal details without reason, though over time she had shared more with Lexi than with anyone else. The time they spent together was usually more light-hearted and fun, even when it included serial killer dramas.

The concern in Lexi's voice reminded Robyn why she didn't often share these things with people. Her stomach turned, and she felt uncomfortable and on display. She got up from her seat quickly, to avoid the pitying look, and spoke to break the too-heavy silence.

"I'm going to grab a drink—do you want anything?"

Instead of replying, Lexi reached out to grab her hand as she passed. Robyn wasn't sure if Lexi intended to stop her or was simply offering a gesture of support, but she was unprepared for the change in trajectory. Before she knew what was happening, she found herself planted in Lexi's lap, with Lexi's arms wrapped around her to stop them both from landing on the floor.

Robyn's face was so close to Lexi's that warm breath grazed across her lips. Her own breathing was laboured as time froze and they stared at each other. Robyn's heart started thumping in her chest and she wondered if Lexi could feel it too. So many thoughts raced across her mind, but one was a clear front-runner. *Kiss her.* She fought against the urge to press her lips to the full, pink ones, so close she could almost taste the watermelon-scented gloss Lexi adored.

Before Robyn could make a mistake that put everything in jeopardy, Lexi started to laugh. The sound filled the air around them, so loud Robyn could feel the vibrations all over her skin. It hit her then that it was a sound she hadn't heard in far too long, one she hadn't realized was missing. She never wanted to go this long without hearing Lexi's laugh again. Robyn's body shook with her own laughter, and she lost her balance, ending up flat on her ass anyway, despite Lexi's attempts to grab her.

Tears rolled down her cheeks as their laughter intensified and Lexi slid down to join her on the floor. Minutes ticked by, and her stomach hurt, but every other part of her was lighter than it had been since the earlier call. She wasn't even sure what they were laughing at anymore, but it didn't matter. The sound would subside for a moment or two, then one of them would look at the other and the silence would be broken as more laughter bubbled out.

As they sat side by side on the cold wooden floor, backs against the couch, Robyn understood how much she had taken for granted the past few years. Robyn's childhood hadn't been perfect, but it had been pretty idyllic for the first twelve years. Which made the loss cut even deeper. She didn't simply lose her father. She lost a house filled with laughter. She lost the way her mom smiled every time her father kissed her goodbye. She lost belief that one day she could find her own happily ever after. But she had spent so long since then working to escape the past, and the memories of everything she had lost, that she had never stopped to fully appreciate all she had gained.

She glanced to where Lexi sat beside her and smiled at the remnants of a smile on Lexi's lips, still ready to break into a laugh at any moment. Their apartment, and Robyn's life, was a much lighter place when filled with the laughter and joy Lexi usually radiated. Robyn was overcome with a need to do everything she could to find a way to help Lexi rediscover her creativity again, for both their sakes.

❖

Why do they call it morning sickness if it's happening at eleven p.m.?

Lexi turned on her side in her queen-size bed, a gift from her parents and the only furniture she had that wasn't second-hand, and grinned at her sister's message.

I don't think it's called morning sickness if you're the one getting sick when your wife is pregnant.

She received a very quick eye roll emoji back followed by Sam's response.

You're hilarious. Brooke's doing the puking, I'm on an emergency ice-cream run.

Puking and ice-cream probably shouldn't go together, but she wasn't one to argue.

Get all the flavours, don't forget last time when you got the wrong one and almost had to sleep on my couch. Hug Brooke for me. See you this weekend.

She put her phone down and rolled over, knowing she needed to sleep but with a head full of thoughts. Being around Sam and Brooke lately made her long for that closeness with someone. She kept replaying her conversation with Sam earlier that week. Was she right? Not only about figuring out the why behind the creative block, but also about not putting the love life stuff on hold. Lexi loved to paint. She loved pouring her passion into art of any kind, from pieces she sold in galleries to her upcycled furniture dotted around the apartment. Until recently, it had fulfilled her in ways that never left time for what-ifs. But since she had begun to struggle to paint anything worthwhile, her life had been feeling a whole lot emptier and her brain a whole lot fuller.

Her thoughts turned to Finley and the little nibling on the way. Did she want kids of her own? It was something she hadn't really stopped to consider before, but now she couldn't shake the idea. She loved spending time with Fin and he adored her just as much. Being an aunt was more rewarding than she'd ever expected. It made her wonder what shaping a tiny human of her own could be like.

She sighed as once again her thoughts took over and sleep lost. She got out of bed, put on a robe, and made her way to her easel in the corner of the room. Paintbrush in hand, she stared at the canvas, willing muscle memory to take over. Some pieces took days, some weeks, some even months. She never minded giving each piece the time it needed, happy to let the ideas swirling around her head take the lead. Her paintings had sold well in local galleries for an up-and-comer. It wasn't a steady income, but with help from her parents while she found her footing, it was enough. She just needed time to let her art make its mark on the world.

That's what she kept telling herself, and her father. But months had turned to years, and she was still just…waiting. Waiting for that big break that would somersault her career. She stopped accepting help from her parents. She was lucky to have their financial support as an option, but the weight of her father's expectations and concerns had become too much to bear. Their relationship had gotten more and more strained by the day, and money wasn't worth destroying that.

Lexi began to pretend she was doing better than she was, pride not allowing her to admit that her father's concerns might have been justified. She wanted his support, but not in the ways he thought were best to give it. She wanted him to believe in her. And she wanted to prove to him that her passion was worth pouring her all into. She couldn't do that when he just saw her as that naive little girl who needed protection.

Waiting for fate to make people see the value of her art wasn't working, and so she eventually opened up to Sam and Brooke about everything. They didn't judge her, pity her, or try to protect her. They discussed options for grants and Lexi applied for a couple with no success. She knew there were plenty more, but finding the motivation to do this kind of paperwork was another type of constant battle. She was an artist and that's what she wanted to be, but the path to her dream seemed to get longer by the day. People weren't falling at her feet to offer her money to sit and paint whatever came to mind, and that long path forward was blocked by mountains of boring forms.

Sam was a graphic designer and she'd worked on Lexi's website to showcase her art and set her up with ways to accept commissions online. Brooke's friend Dani was an artist too, who was gracious enough to send some contacts Lexi's way. Soon enough, orders started to trickle in.

Before then, Lexi had only ever painted what was in her head, never fully knowing how a piece would end up until it was done. The first few orders were for private buyers, and the excitement of being sought out to paint what they wanted spurred her on. A couple were for gifts, so the buyer gave some basic details and Lexi had the freedom to create unique pieces for them. It was exciting, to get a glimpse into other people's lives and see their happiness when she produced their requests.

Eventually, she started getting requests with stricter requirements. Clients had a vision, without the artistic talents to create it themselves, so they came to her. The pieces she produced based on their guidance weren't her usual style, but the customers were happy, and she was finally making enough money to live, not just survive. Her reputation started to develop, just like she had hoped.

Then a larger company reached out. They wanted to order a set of paintings for their newly opened office from a local artist. Their offices were modern, and they prided themselves on being unique and authentic, even though the description of what they wanted was unimaginative and trite. The company's vision was very different from her usual paintings, but the money was more than her pieces had ever sold for in the past. So, she agreed. This was what she had worked toward, right? Earning a living doing what she loved.

Except she wasn't doing what she loved anymore. The first deadline came and went, and the company extended it. Lexi used an excuse about issues with supplies, which wasn't a total lie but wasn't the whole truth. The truth was she had absolutely no desire to produce the boring, unoriginal pieces they had asked for and she had no idea how to do it without that desire. People worked every day doing things they didn't enjoy and yet they still managed to do their jobs. So why couldn't she just do it?

The worst part was this creative block wasn't just affecting her ability to paint these pieces. It had drained her inspiration and motivation completely. She tried painting anything to get back into the swing of things, but she had set up everything daily the past few weeks and nothing ever came from it. She was exactly three weeks from her final deadline, and if she couldn't produce the pieces she had agreed upon, the company would rightfully cancel her contract.

They weren't artists, or even art connoisseurs, who understood things like this. They didn't care about the creative process or blocks—they cared about getting what they ordered. The weight on Lexi's shoulders wouldn't budge as she dipped her paintbrush into the nearest colour on her palette absentmindedly, dragging the liquid acrylic paint across the canvas in a frustrated swipe. Tears threatened to fall as the angry red line dripped down the white linen material. She dipped the same brush into the black paint, not bothering to grab a new one and swiped again.

An angry X glared back at her as the colours bled into one

another. The lines blurred as the tears fell down her cheeks and she dropped the brush onto the paint-splattered sheet beneath her. Her shoulders shook as she sobbed until strong arms wrapped around her. The unmistakable scent of smoke that always lingered on Robyn's skin after a busy shift filled Lexi's nostrils. She turned in Robyn's embrace and sobbed against the cotton fabric of her hoodie. They stayed like that long after Lexi's tears subsided. Robyn didn't ask questions and just allowed Lexi to fall apart in the safety of her arms, only uttering one sentence the whole time.

"I've got you, Sunny."

CHAPTER FOUR

The silence was interrupted by soft sniffles as Robyn held Lexi close, glad to have gotten home when she did. Her heart panged with sadness and a persistent itch to fix whatever caused the tears that flowed down Lexi's cheeks. Because that's what Robyn did. When there was a problem to be fixed, she fixed it, and Lexi's mood lately was definitely a problem. It was one thing to feel frustrated by a creative block, but the sadness she was witnessing concerned Robyn. She hadn't thought twice about walking right over to pull Lexi into her arms. As Lexi's body shook and tears stained Robyn's hoodie, she wanted nothing more than to find the joy that Lexi so freely shared with the world and give it back to her.

Minutes passed as Robyn ran a soothing hand up and down Lexi's back. When Lexi pulled away and wiped quickly at her cheeks, it took everything in Robyn not to reach out and tug her back in.

"I'm sorry. I just…it's been a long day. I should sleep. Sorry."

Lexi mumbled as she moved, walking past Robyn toward her room.

"Wait, Sunny. You don't have anything to apologize for. Do you want to talk? Can I help?"

She could hear the borderline pleading tone of her voice and wondered if Lexi noticed it too.

"You did help. I'm okay. I just need sleep. Thanks, Robbie."

Lexi didn't look back as she spoke, continuing into her room and shutting the door behind her. Robyn stood staring at the door, hoping it would open again and Lexi would come back out. Not that she knew what she would do if that happened. The only thing she knew is she wanted to help. To do something to bring that smile back to Lexi's face.

She paced their living room and racked her mind with ways to cheer Lexi up. Almost everywhere in their small apartment held things Lexi had found in second-hand shops or they had sourced together at car boot sales. Most were improved upon by Lexi's creative touch in one way or another. Lexi's bread and butter were paintings, and even with Robyn's novice understanding she could tell Lexi was damn good at them, but her creative abilities extended far beyond the pieces that hung on gallery walls.

It had been far too long since she'd seen Lexi try to work on anything other than a blank canvas. That's when it hit her. She grabbed her phone and scrolled through social media until she found what she was looking for. There was a car boot sale on tomorrow, an hour's drive from them. She hoped it would bring some of the inspiration Lexi was clearly missing. As she dragged herself to bed after making her plan, she grimaced at the time. Her alarm showed four hours until it would sound as she set it for the next morning.

She had barely fallen into a restless sleep before it went off again. She knew Lexi would want to get there early, so she forced herself to wake up. She grabbed her phone to silence the beeping alarm and groaned at the time. It was far too early to be awake, let alone out of bed, on her day off. But she had a good reason, she reminded herself, as she rolled over and forced her legs onto the floor. Opening the dark green curtains, she took in the pale blue sky as hints of the early morning sun glinted off the glass. At least the weather forecast had predicted correctly—her plan would be less than ideal if the typical Irish rain showed up.

She dressed quickly in comfortable black linen pants, a fire brigade charity T-shirt from the last fundraising event where she had retained her rope climbing record, and the years-old grey hoodie she always wore when she had to be up early. It was soft and cosy, with fleece lining on the inside, and it made her feel like she was taking a little bit of her bed with her wherever she went. Especially comforting when she was hesitant to leave bed in the first place.

She made her way into the kitchen and boiled the kettle. She grabbed two travel mugs from the cupboard and dropped a tea bag into each. She listened for any sign that she had woken Lexi as she set about making the tea to their respective liking. This included far too much sugar for Lexi. After the mugs were filled and the bag was packed with snacks and water, she channelled her inner Lexi and bounded into the bedroom to her right.

"Time to get up, let's go!"

Lexi jerked awake as Robyn landed on her bed, in a perfect replica of Lexi's usual enthusiasm. Robyn had woken many a morning to Lexi buzzing with palpable excitement, packed and ready for a car boot sale that Robyn had begrudgingly agreed to bring her to. Lexi had sold her car a couple of years ago, since it had spent most of the time parked up in the shared car park for their apartment complex. Although cars weren't a necessity in the city, Robyn couldn't part with hers. She loved the freedom of being able to hop in and drive to clear her mind whenever she needed to. Plus, with her varying shift times, there wasn't always public transport available when she got off from work.

So, Lexi often commandeered her car, along with her strength, to carry and transport the various second-hand items she scored. They could range from tiny trinkets right up to the large oak dresser currently taking up most of Lexi's bedroom wall. That one had been a challenge and required reinforcements in the way of Lexi's father's van. Despite Robyn's grumpiness about the early morning starts, she always enjoyed the time with Lexi rooting through stalls and trying to get the best bargains.

Lexi's forehead creased in confusion as she took in Robyn, fully dressed and bouncing on her bed.

"Wh-what's going on? What's wrong?"

Robyn didn't have to fake her smile or enthusiasm. Lexi looked far too cute in her sleep-addled state as she rubbed her eyes. It was almost worth the early rise to take this in.

"Up, Sunny. We're going to be late!"

Robyn was being deliberately evasive. She knew with the mood Lexi had been in lately, she would've declined Robyn's offer to go had she discussed it with her first and pitched it as an idea. Instead, she was going with the tactic of compelled fun. It was a risk, but Robyn was low on ideas, and patience wasn't her strong suit. She needed to take action.

By some miracle, Lexi listened to her and reluctantly rolled out of bed. She had always been more of a morning person than Robyn, who would have demanded exact details and lengthy reasoning behind why she had to get up before the sun had fully risen if their roles were reversed. Robyn took in Lexi's colourful pyjamas. She lifted her gaze slowly up the bare midsection on display as Lexi stretched, the thin fabric of her top riding up dangerously high. Robyn glanced away, hoping Lexi hadn't noticed her wandering eyes or flushed cheeks.

"So which car boot sale are you pity driving me to?"

Robyn's face fell, her element of surprise quashed. Lexi had an innate way of knowing things, despite Robyn's lack of sharing. It was a unique quality that Robyn was thankful for when she didn't feel up to discussing something and resented at times like this when she was unable to keep anything a surprise.

"How did you know?" Robyn heard her own whine and tempered it with her next sentence. "I didn't say a thing about a car boot sale."

She sounded a little like her youngest niece with her petulant tone when she was denying something she most certainly had done. Lexi's mouth lifted in a small smile, and she nodded toward Robyn.

"You're wearing your car boot sale hoodie. You also witnessed me be a sobbing mess last night and you were pacing the living room obviously scheming before I fell asleep. I put the pieces together."

How those pieces fit together in a way that led Lexi to correctly assume her intentions was a little eerie. Robyn was trained to look out for the little things, and even she wasn't sure she would have gathered as much from these few clues.

"I really appreciate you trying to cheer me up, Robbie, but it's your day off. You should be relaxing."

Robyn walked over and reached out for Lexi before she could think too much about it, pulling her in for a quick hug. The vulnerability on Lexi's face had made Robyn's body move before her mind caught up. She stepped back before she had time to second-guess herself and was happy to see some of the tension had ebbed from Lexi's shoulders.

"I'll relax when we're finding more weird shit that you somehow make beautiful and unique. This isn't up for debate. I've got the bag packed, tea in cups, and we need to be on the road in ten. So, get dressed and let's go have some fun!"

Lexi's eyebrows rose as Robyn's voice took on an uncharacteristically upbeat tone, but it worked. Robyn exited the room as Lexi started to grab clothes. The small smile that Lexi shot at her on her way out made Robyn's exhaustion dissipate, and her stomach filled with butterflies.

Oh, shit. Not good.

❖

A little over an hour later, after a pit stop to grab takeaway breakfast rolls at a local deli, they reached their destination right on time. Lexi sipped from the insulated travel mug in her hand as they pulled into the car park already filled with eager customers. There were a couple of familiar faces dotted around and it was comforting to know some things hadn't changed. Car boot sales tended to pull in a few regulars, those that travelled around to source bargains and always showed up early.

Some, like Lexi, loved finding something old and making it their own. They would arrive early to make a day of it and take their time, the way she did, to really source out the gems that to another might look worthless. Others would search for whatever they considered valuable enough to sell later and make more money out of. She had often seen people purchase things that would crop up on their own stalls at a later car boot sale with a hefty markup. Once or twice, she'd even witnessed it happen on the same day.

Couples and families looking for something to do in the rare dry weather would venture out later in the day, happy to look at what was on offer at their leisure. She took in the familiar scene and her chest squeezed in conflict. She was worried that it wouldn't bring the usual joy it held for her, and she would lose another comfort in her life. But when Robyn sat on her bed looking at her with hopeful eyes, she couldn't say no.

It was so out of character for Robyn to not only willingly attend, but to organise the trip. There was no chance Lexi would turn her down. She gripped the mug tighter as they climbed out of the car and the heat against her palm reminded her that Robyn had also been thoughtful enough to make her tea, pack a bag of snacks, and pick a place for breakfast on the way. She had gone to a lot of effort for Lexi. That in itself was enough to loosen the coil in her chest.

Robyn was pulling her hair into a messy ponytail and Lexi studied her face for a moment. Her cool porcelain skin was dotted with seasonal freckles across both cheeks. Her dark brown eyes were framed by long black lashes. Robyn was beautiful by any standard, but today there was something about her eager, hopeful look with a hint of uncertainty, that made her face glow. Lexi almost couldn't look away.

Robyn was acting nervous. It was so different from the usual self-assured, nonchalant attitude Lexi was used to. It was intriguing in a way Lexi couldn't describe. She never had a doubt Robyn cared about her. They had grown close in the past few years, as close as Robyn let anyone. If she needed anything, all she had to do was ask and Robyn would do whatever she could to help, even if it was done with grumbling and furrowed brows. But this was different. Lexi hadn't asked. This was all Robyn's doing, and that was new.

As they made their way into the open field, dotted with rows of tables, Lexi veered right to one at the front covered with bric-a-brac. As she searched among the piles, a calm washed over her that was replaced with excitement at the bargains she discovered. She started to make a pile as she heard a soft chuckle beside her.

"It's only the start, Lex, you might want to save room in your bags."

Lexi, of course, ignored Robyn's advice, and they fell into a comfortable rhythm for the morning. Robyn was back to her usual grumbling and sarcasm once Lexi relaxed, happiness evident on her face and in her weighted-down bags. Most of which Robyn carried, so Lexi's hands were free in her search for more.

They made their way to the car after a fruitful few hours and loaded the bags inside. Robyn joined Lexi where she leaned against the closed boot to take a gulp of water, enjoying the light breeze that surrounded them.

"My feet are vibrating, and my arms are dead."

Lexi laughed, turning her head at Robyn's words.

"You're a firefighter. Yet a little light walking and carrying a few bags is what does you in?"

Robyn scowled, standing up straighter.

"Me and you have very different definitions of light walk. And of *few*, for that matter. Are you planning to completely redecorate our apartment, or what?"

Lexi shrugged as they made their way inside the car.

"Maybe. Some are gifts. I had an idea for a hand-made rainbow mobile with some of the pieces I picked up that would be perfect for Sam and Brooke's nursery."

Lexi paused at the look on Robyn's face, a mixture of relief and smugness.

"What? What's that look about?"

Robyn faced forward and started to drive before replying.

"It's nice to hear you talk about your ideas. Clearly *my* idea was a good one."

Lexi relaxed back in the chair, refusing to allow the anxiety that had been haunting her every creative thought room to creep back in.

"Don't get too cocky yet. I haven't actually made anything. They are just ideas."

But despite her words, Lexi was hopeful. They were just ideas. But ideas had been escaping her for far too long now, so even the hint of them was a start.

"I've seen what you can do with your ideas, Sunny. So my cockiness stands. That sounded weirder out loud than it did in my head."

Lexi turned her head as she grinned at Robyn. Her stomach flipped, an unfamiliar sensation lately. She was feeling so much more positive than she had in a long time, and it was all thanks to the person sitting right beside her. She reached out softly before she even thought about it and squeezed Robyn's hand where it sat on the gear stick.

"Thanks, Robbie. Really. You don't know how much this meant to me."

Robyn's hand tensed a little beneath Lexi's, and then relaxed.

"No worries, Lex. Plus, you're buying me lunch."

CHAPTER FIVE

R obyn sat in a booth across from Lexi at the café where they had stopped to get the lunch she had jokingly demanded and Lexi had eventually insisted upon. They had finished eating and were now trying to decide whether to get dessert or not. It was early, but time wasn't real anyway, right? Or so she told herself as she eyed up the chocolate brownie on the menu.

"You might as well take advantage of me while you can."

Robyn almost choked on the badly timed sip of water she had taken as it slid back in her throat. Lexi raised both eyebrows in surprised amusement before speaking again.

"Since I'm buying and all…"

Oh, yes, dessert. She meant dessert. Robyn's cheeks heated as she lifted the menu up in pretence to give herself time to cool down. Taking advantage of Lexi brought very different things to mind, thoughts Robyn had absolutely no business thinking. When the waiter approached, she ordered a dessert just to prove to Lexi she had been reviewing the menu and not hiding behind it suspiciously. And yes, because the brownie sounded amazing.

Her phone beeped as the waiter left with their order and she groaned as she read the message lighting her screen. She met Lexi's quizzical stare and explained.

"My mom. She's badgering me again about a date for the anniversary party. How she thinks I'm going to start dating someone within a few days is anyone's guess. Someone I would invite to meet my whole family."

Robyn's shoulders slumped as she pictured the disappointment that would mar her mother's features when she showed up alone, again.

"Just tell her that. She'll have to understand."

Robyn laughed mirthlessly.

"You don't know my mother like I do. I'm well adept at disappointing her, I've been doing that for long enough."

Their dessert arrived, and even the decadent chocolate square wouldn't shift the dark cloud that had descended above her head.

"You've mentioned before about her being disappointed in you. I know the feeling in some ways—I constantly worry my dad's disappointed because I'm not in what he considers a stable job. But you are. You're in a job that helps people every day and you have a good circle of people around you. What's there to be disappointed by?"

Robyn scrambled for the words to explain the conversations that outwardly looked like any normal parental curiosities, but inwardly opened wounds that had never fully healed.

"You know my dad was a firefighter too. When I told my mom I was training for the job, I thought maybe she would be proud of me. Following in my father's footsteps, you know? I knew she would be worried. He died on the job, so it made sense she might not want that for me. But ultimately, I figured I'd be doing something she knew he would be proud of me for."

Lexi nodded, encouraging Robyn to go on.

"But instead of pride or worry or anger I just got… nothing. She looked at me, but she was looking right through me. I know that doesn't make sense, but that's the only way I can describe it. It was like she hadn't even registered my words. Her response was to ask me if I'd met anyone yet."

Robyn wanted to explain to Lexi that it wasn't so much what her mother said, it was all the things she didn't say, that created these holes in Robyn. Silences that brought her right back to all those years ago when her father had died and her mother had been so devastated by grief. That version of her mother who spent her days doing the mom things she had always done, but with a new quietness that was louder than any noise Robyn had ever heard. Her mother's grief and silence had slowly melted away, but the glimpses of sorrow and disappointment Robyn caught during their conversations were enough to bring her own grief right back.

"The thing is, I'm never going to walk in my father's footsteps because not only was he a firefighter, a hero, he also managed to have a wife and kids who adored him. His life was full, and it feels like to her, mine is empty. Maybe I'm making assumptions, and I should just confront my mom with this. But it took a long time after my dad died for me to really understand the impact of being a walking reminder of him, and those are things I'm still working through."

"That must be hard. I can't pretend I totally understand, so I won't tell you to just talk to her about it. You need to get there in your own time. But your life is far from empty, Robbie."

Lexi reached out and placed a hand over Robyn's, squeezing briefly as Robyn replied.

"I just wish for once I could go and enjoy spending time with my family, without having to face her clipped comments and questioning."

"I could go."

Robyn glanced up at Lexi's words.

"Bringing you would probably just provoke her more. I

can just hear her. *You have time for playing house with your friends, but not for love.* Plus, she'll spend the night trying to set you up with one of my cousins and I promise you, you don't want that."

Lexi laughed at Robyn, but her next words stopped the cake laden fork from reaching Robyn's mouth.

"So…pretend we're more than friends. It would get your mother off your back for a while and save me from her playing Cupid. Plus, it could be fun. Your sisters always ask if we're dating anyway, no matter how many times you say we're just roommates, so you may as well use it to your advantage."

Robyn finally got the cake into her mouth before it fell, and chewed slowly as she considered Lexi's suggestion. Could she really bring Lexi to the party as her fake girlfriend? Would her mother even buy it? Maybe, if she pretended she hadn't told her sooner because she didn't know if it would work out or not. It was a ridiculous idea, but once it took root, she couldn't shake it. Her mother was so desperate for her to start dating that she would probably accept any story Robyn spun, regardless of how ridiculous.

"You'd be my fake girlfriend and put up with my whole family thinking we're together? Possibly questioning why you're suddenly not straight? They have zero tact, especially for things that aren't their business."

Lexi cocked her head to the side and regarded Robyn a little too intensely for her liking.

"Firstly, I never said I was straight. To your family, or to you. Secondly, you kidnapped me into having fun today. I feel more alive, more excited to go home and create, than I have in a long time. So yes, I will absolutely be the best fake girlfriend you've ever had. By the time I'm done, your mother will be planning our wedding without a hint of disappointment."

Robyn mumbled that she'd think about Lexi's offer, but the whole time her brain was working overtime. Her heart had flipped at all of Lexi's words, but one line in particular had her stomach in knots and heat creeping back up her neck and face. If Lexi noticed, she didn't comment, as they finished their dessert. The sentence ran through Robyn's mind the whole drive home as she manoeuvred the car around the familiar streets on autopilot. Luckily, Lexi remained equally silent, caught up with her own thoughts by the faraway look on her face.

I never said I was straight.

Robyn shook her head. Was Lexi kidding? Could that be true? She racked her brain back to when they first met, after Lexi answered Robyn's ad on the rental website for a roommate. Had they discussed her sexuality then? Lexi was dating Ethan at the time. They broke up shortly after she moved in, so Robyn hadn't gotten to know him well. Had she assumed? Had she fallen into the trap of judging Lexi's sexuality based on who she was dating?

Robyn couldn't get past the fact that, if Lexi was serious, this was a monumental piece of information that she should have known. How had it never come up before? Robyn was one of the first people Lexi confided in when she learned about her sister. Even after meeting Sam, when she told Robyn about the similarities between them, she hadn't mentioned her own sexuality at all despite mentioning that Sam was a lesbian. Did it matter? Why was she so hung up on this?

She asked herself that several times throughout the rest of the day, but the answer was one she was afraid to admit. Her crush, longing, curiosity, whatever you wanted to call it, had been easy to ignore when it was aimed at her straight, unavailable roommate. It was a lot harder to push it to the side when suddenly her whole view of Lexi was shifted on its axis, including the potential that maybe, just maybe, Lexi wasn't so unavailable after all.

❖

Why had she said that?

The words swam in circles around Lexi's head as she lay in bed staring at the ceiling, the glow from her lamp casting a shadow along the white paint. The rest of the day had passed in a blur after their conversation at lunch that had taken a turn she hadn't been prepared for. After they returned to their apartment, both she and Robyn had spent the afternoon avoiding the elephant in the room.

She busied herself sorting through her car boot sale purchases, coming up with ideas for the mobile and getting to work on the basic structure of it. Although the beginning was more engineering than creativity, she was happy with the progress she had made so far, nonetheless. Robyn had even helped with drilling some of the holes Lexi would need to fit the smaller strings through as she wanted to avoid using glue. Kids tended to get their hands on the things they were definitely not supposed to get their hands on far too often, so although it was for room decor, she wanted this mobile to be as baby-proof as possible.

They existed in relative silence most of the day, Robyn reading on the couch next to her as Lexi worked. Although the silence was palpable at times, it was calming to have someone near her without expectation of conversation. She got lost in her mind as she sketched her ideas for the mobile. Every now and then, she'd glance over and notice Robyn's eyes on her. They'd exchange a smile before Robyn diverted her eyes back to her book, and warmth would surround Lexi, her own smile lingering as she continued her activity.

But now, in the dim light and silence of her room, the conversation at lunch was stuck on repeat in her mind. She groaned as she replayed the words again and pushed her face into the pillow as if to block out the sound of her own thoughts.

I never said I was straight.

While technically true, Lexi couldn't fathom why the words had left her mouth in that context. It was something she acknowledged to herself occasionally but hadn't yet uttered aloud. Relationships were so far from her mind after her break-up with Ethan that her sexuality was never something she wanted to spend much time trying to figure out. The longer she had gone without addressing it, the stranger it would have been to announce something without cause.

Hey, Robyn, I think I might be something other than straight. I'm not hitting on you or telling you because you're gay, but I felt the need to announce it.

Nothing was ever the right approach. Plus, people never announced they were straight, so why should she have to announce that she wasn't? She was lucky enough to be confident of support from the closest people in her life if she began to date someone other than a man. Her parents had always set an example for her of the safety they would provide to anyone who needed it, something she had never doubted.

On top of that, they now adored Sam and Brooke almost as much as she did. Finley had gained not only an aunt, but two new pseudo-grandparents. Lexi was completely comfortable with the fact that her sexuality would be a non-issue for her parents. Both her sister and roommate were gay, so they hadn't been a concern, and anyone else's opinion didn't matter enough to be a factor.

It wasn't fear that stopped her from exploring that side of herself; up until now it had mostly been indifference. She'd begun to date Ethan because he'd asked, not because she had a burning desire to be with him. Was it love at first sight? No. But over time, as they got closer as friends, her feelings blossomed into something resembling what she had read about in books and watched on TV. So, when he asked her out, she'd agreed, and they had been happy together for a time. She hadn't spent the time pining after girls or wishing she didn't have to kiss him. She'd enjoyed sex when they were together, but it wasn't something she thought much about when it wasn't happening.

She always had the niggling feeling that it couldn't be right, he couldn't be the one. Because it wasn't the instant, all consuming passion she had been promised by the media for her whole childhood. She had put it down to art taking up most of the passion she possessed, coupled with the fact that they were young when they met. Lexi knew she wasn't a lesbian. It had been a consideration for a while, especially when she wondered if that was why she didn't feel the attraction for Ethan right from the start, or any man for that matter. But she could never remember feeling instant attraction to any women either.

When she stumbled upon the term *demisexual* online, while scrolling through social media one day, pieces started to click into place and her feelings made more sense. She wasn't sure where exactly her attraction lay when it came to gender, but she hadn't cared enough to find out, figuring it would make itself known when the time came for it to matter. But having a name for the way her feelings surfaced allowed her to put those niggling questions at bay for a while. She wasn't straight, and that was okay. It might become relevant to share that information sometime, it might not.

So why had she shared that with Robyn now? Why had it

been so important to state in that moment? It wasn't something she had actively hidden before, and she'd never explicitly said she was straight, but she thought Robyn assumed so. She never felt the need to correct her, until today. After the words left Robyn's lips, Lexi didn't want her to continue with that assumption. Maybe because not correcting it when the words were out there would feel like a lie, more so than if the assumption was unsaid. Or maybe for reasons Lexi wasn't ready to address even to herself yet.

Lexi's eyes were heavy, and exhaustion from the early morning hit her without warning. Her phone beeped from its place on her nightstand, and she reached out to click into the notification. She read the message under Robyn's name and smiled before her lids began to fall as the tiredness took over.

Okay, you're on. Party is Saturday at 8 pm. Thanks, Sunny. Love, your favourite fake girlfriend.

Her heart fluttered softly, and she fell into a sleep filled with dreams of deep brown eyes, freckled cheeks, and a smile that filled her with hope.

CHAPTER SIX

So let me get this straight, Red. You're taking your roommate, who's definitely just a friend, to your sister's wedding anniversary as your fake girlfriend. And you're doing this to appease your mother so she'll stop badgering you about dating? And what then, do you just fake date your roommate forever? Are you gonna get fake married and have fake babies or is that where we draw a line?"

When Tommy said it like that, a knot formed in Robyn's stomach at the idea of her sister's wedding anniversary the next day. That she would be attending with Lexi. It was a silly idea. Why had Lexi suggested it? Why had she agreed? Sending that message to Lexi had been a spur-of-the-moment decision. After the weird way their afternoon ended, she wanted to let her know things were okay. Whether Lexi had been making a sarcastic comeback or whether she had confided something important to Robyn was still up in the air. *Except it isn't really, is it?* Robyn knew Lexi better than to think she would joke about something like that. If Lexi said it, she meant it.

Robyn wanted to show Lexi that she was fine with who she was, whatever that amounted to. Clearly, her method of doing so was a bit unorthodox. *Be my fake girlfriend* screamed *I'm cool if you're not straight*, right? She chewed her food slowly, too slowly, considering the alarm could ring at any moment and she could go hungry for the rest of her shift. The nausea in her stomach wasn't helping her appetite, and the questioning from Tommy made her want to climb into her bunk and pull the blanket over her head, hunger be damned.

"There's no point in reminding me it's a ridiculous idea. I already told my mother that I'm bringing Lexi, so there's no going back now. You should've heard her, Brenn. It was like a switch flipped."

Her mom's change of tone toward her had been immediately noticeable. There was a new warmth in her words as she gushed about Lexi and always knowing how well they were suited for one another. It was true that her family often told her how lucky she would be to find a girl like Lexi. It was part of the reason she'd avoided inviting them over.

"She's just happy you're giving up your lesbian lothario ways, Robbie. No parent wants that, even the most understanding of them."

Robyn sighed. "I don't want you making sense of her, Brenn, just let me vent."

"Cool, cool. Let's go." He shook out his hands and turned fully to face her. "You're right. She should be supportive of your many one-night stands and inability to form romantic attachments. Like all normal parents are." His deadpan expression had Robyn laughing despite herself.

"You're not helpful. I don't need her to be okay with how I spend my free time. But I tell her I have a date and she uses words like *happy* and *proud*, something that hasn't happened in far too long. Going into dangerous situations daily to save people's lives isn't enough to make her proud, but now that I found myself a date, that's what does it?"

Robyn's voice rose at the end, exasperation leaking out of every word. The problem was, *proud* was being thrown around in ways that had Robyn craving more and hating herself a little for it.

"She's your weak spot, Red. I've never known you to care what anybody thinks about you. Anyone except your mother. She gets under your skin quicker with one message than any of us ever have, even when we fuck up on a job."

Tommy was right. Her mother was Robyn's weak spot and she knew it. Robyn lived her life in a way that made her feel good about herself, and that's what mattered. She was proud of the job she did. She loved the feeling it gave her. She got to go home every night knowing she made a difference in people's lives. That some people had those lives in part because of her and her colleagues. Even the times they dealt with minor incidents, it still mattered. She was important to the people around her.

She blew off steam in ways that some might look down upon, but that had never bothered her. She didn't have time for dating, and she enjoyed sex. One didn't have to be the only way to get the other. She found like-minded people and shared their company and they parted mutually satisfied, without emotional complications. Her job was dangerous. She didn't want someone at home waiting for her, resenting her, filled with worry whenever they heard about a big fire on the news.

"She doesn't make any sense. She's so proud I'm dating, like she forgets how that ended for her. I don't want to turn someone else into a shell of themselves if I don't come home one day." *The way my mother did*, Robyn added in her head.

Her job wasn't something she was willing to compromise on, even for love. People looked up to her. She walked into the fire station and had the respect of her colleagues. She was the one new recruits came to with questions. The one people relied on to know what was happening and to have the answers.

She solved problems both on calls and in the fire station, and she did it without making people feel bad for having those problems to begin with. Those qualities were the reason she was up for promotion.

They were also all the qualities her mother glossed over and disregarded. Respect wasn't something Robyn felt from her mother, not in longer than she could recall. Robyn wished it didn't matter to her. That she could shrug it off, like she did any judgement from the rest of her family.

"I know you said not to make sense of it, but she's from a different time, Red. She has different values. And those are values you don't share anyway, so you need to find a way to make peace with not living up to them. Her expectations are on her, not you."

Robyn nodded along because everything Tommy said made sense. Yet there was still that part of her clinging to the hope that maybe things would change if her mom finally *saw* her.

A tiny glimmer of hope thought that maybe this fake date would allow that to happen. It would put an end to the relentless conversations about her settling down, at least for a while, and allow her mother time to see the important things about Robyn. The things others appreciated, rather than the things Robyn lacked that took up most of their stilted conversations. Robyn couldn't turn around now and say, no, there is no date. She couldn't face the disappointment after getting a taste of how it felt to hear pride in her mother's voice.

The rest of the shift flew by. Tommy laid off teasing her about it, which meant her face wasn't doing a good job at concealing how much it really meant to her. She and Tommy made fun of each other daily, that was their thing. They didn't take things too seriously most of the time—the job was serious enough without them adding to it. But she knew he loved her like a sister, and she trusted him with her life. Just not her deepest insecurities. Those she kept locked up tight.

❖

Lexi wrung her hands together and then shook them out, staring at herself in the full-length mirror at the front of her wardrobe. Why was she so nervous? It wasn't like she'd never met Robyn's family before. She had met most of her extended family at Robyn's surprise thirtieth birthday party a couple of years ago, which Robyn's sister April had thrown and Robyn had absolutely hated.

Lexi had even been the person tasked with getting Robyn there, under the guise of a quiet dinner out to celebrate Lexi's fictional achievement. She couldn't even remember what excuse she had used, but it worked, and she was sure a tiny part of Robyn had never forgiven her, despite Robyn's assurances that her wrath was solely aimed at her family.

She had partied with the same people who would be in attendance tonight, and she knew they would be nice to her. She enjoyed parties most of the time. Seeing people happy and celebrating always made her skin buzz with empathetic excitement. Right now however, her skin was buzzing with more nerves than she had felt in a while. This time was different. She was being introduced as Robyn's date. She would have to act like Robyn's girlfriend in a way that was believable enough to fool Robyn's mother.

Her stomach flipped at the thought as a soft knock sounded on her door. She took a last glance at her soft pink dress that fell right above her knee. It was one of her favourites. The elastic waistband made dancing comfortable while the crossover V neckline dipped low enough to be sensual while still being family party appropriate. Her blond hair was clipped up at the back and fell loosely over her shoulder to one side. She bit her lip nervously, knowing she would have to replace her gloss due to the action.

At the second, louder knock she acknowledged the sound and grabbed her clutch purse. She slipped on her strappy white kitten heel sandals and made her way to the living room. Robyn paced the floor outside her bedroom in a dark grey linen pantsuit that clung to her body like it was tailored for her. The black top beneath the blazer was simple yet sophisticated and matched the lace black belt that was more decoration than necessity.

Robyn froze, eyes roaming over her body. The little gulp Robyn made somehow steadied Lexi's nerves and brought a small smile to her lips. The dress had been a good choice.

"You look hot, Sunny."

Hearing those words from anyone else would usually render one of two reactions: embarrassment or discomfort. However, the way Robyn stated it was so matter of fact, without a hint of suggestion, that it made Lexi feel neither of those things. She laughed as Robyn followed the statement up with an over-exaggerated bow. Lexi curtsied in return, going along with the apparent roles they had fallen into.

"You don't look so bad yourself."

Lexi tilted her head in amusement as Robyn held out an elbow to her with a flourish. "Ready for our fake date, darling?"

Lexi linked her arm through Robyn's as they made their way to the door.

"Are we fake dating back in Victorian times?"

Robyn led them to the taxi which was already awaiting them outside. She was determined to stay in chivalrous character as she opened Lexi's door and waved her inside.

"I believe it's called courting, young lady. Plus, chivalry emerged in mediaeval times."

Lexi's nerves completely dissipated as she laughed at Robyn's silliness. It was easier to fall into these ridiculously exaggerated roles because then it was obvious they were acting. Playing a part. No room for confusion.

"I'm only like four years your junior. I'm not sure that warrants young lady status. Plus, the lady part is questionable at least sixty percent of the time."

"Only sixty?"

Lexi caught Robyn's upturned mouth as she shoved her lightly. The rest of the journey was quiet. It seemed more like two rather than the twenty minutes it took them to get to the restaurant. As they pulled up outside the venue, Robyn's hand landed on the exposed skin of Lexi's shaking knee in a reassuring squeeze. So, maybe the nerves hadn't completely dissipated after all.

They exited the car and made their way inside. They were only five minutes late, which was early in Lexi time. The room was already full. Robyn's family had booked out the small restaurant for the occasion, and there were plenty of them to fill it. Lexi looked down in surprise as Robyn's hand slid into hers. Then she remembered they were dating, and holding hands was a normal couple thing to do. She needed to remember that.

Robyn's grip tightened in hers and Lexi glanced up to see Robyn's eyes focused ahead intently. Lexi followed her eyeline to where it landed on Robyn's mom, Marie. With her short stature, light brown hair, and blue eyes, you wouldn't immediately get the familial connection between Robyn and her mother. Robyn's sisters bore a striking resemblance to Marie, but Robyn was the outlier.

About a year after they'd moved into their apartment, Marie had invited Lexi for dinner. When she'd arrived at the house, there was a beautiful photo of Robyn's parents' wedding hanging in the hallway, and it became obvious whom Robyn took after.

Robyn's father had the exact same jet-black hair, albeit shorter. His deep brown eyes were like Robyn's, and it was clear where Robyn got her height, compared to her much shorter siblings. Robyn had come up beside Lexi that night as she inspected the photo and smiled mirthlessly. Then, as they gazed at the photo together, she had mumbled some words Lexi had never forgotten. "Now you know why my mother always has that haunted look around me. I'm his ghost."

The thing was, Robyn wasn't wrong. She wasn't imagining things because Lexi had seen it too. Robyn's mother did treat her differently to her sisters. Not badly, as such, but almost wearily.

Marie spotted them as they made their way farther into the restaurant, and beelined toward them. As she descended upon them, Robyn's hand squeezed hers again. Lexi glanced at her anxious features and squeezed back. The surprised look on her face told Lexi that the original grip had been an unconscious action, but Robyn held tight as if bracing herself. Lexi was overcome with an urge to protect Robyn from the emotional whirlwind these events held for her. Robyn deserved to relax with her family and enjoy herself. Lexi wanted to see the lines on Robyn's forehead disappear and the half-smile she knew so well grace Robyn's lips.

Before thinking more about it, Lexi freed her hand from Robyn's. Lexi could've sworn she glimpsed a shadow of disappointment crossing Robyn's features before her eyes widened as Lexi slid her arm across Robyn's back. She pressed closer to Robyn's side in an intimate gesture, and Robyn's arm snaked around her shoulder as Marie stood in front of them. Lexi thought they probably looked very much the part of a newly smitten couple.

As Robyn chatted to her more-animated-than-usual mother, Lexi took notice of how well they fit together. She was pressed beneath Robyn's arm, and she could feel Robyn's fingers absentmindedly stroking the bare skin of her shoulder. And Lexi was far more comfortable than she should have been. It wasn't like they had never been physically close. They often hugged, or she'd end up resting against Robyn while they watched TV. None of that had ever felt like this. Clearly, she was getting very in character, Lexi told herself. All the while willing the somersaults in her stomach to take a break.

CHAPTER SEVEN

It was a couple of hours into the party and Robyn felt lighter than she had in a very long time, at least while in the presence of the majority of her family. There were a lot of them. She had fifteen aunts and uncles when you combined both sides, which led to a lot of cousins. Not all attended, but there were the usuals milling about. Her sister Ava was popular, always had been, and it was for good reason.

Despite their differences in both looks and personality, Robyn had adored Ava from the first day her mom walked through the door with her. Or so she was told, considering she was only three at the time. For as long as Robyn could remember, Ava had been sweet, kind, and caring. Even when April came along, Ava didn't seem to get any hint of middle child syndrome. She always had a little glow inside her that she was happy to pass on to anyone that needed it, Robyn included, on more occasions than she could count. Robyn was jealous of Ava's relationship with their mom, but she could never hold it against her.

Lexi's hand brushed against Robyn's as she returned from getting them drinks. Ava and Lexi were a lot alike. Rays of sunshine in human form. Robyn smiled at Lexi and tried to tune back into her niece Fiadh's animated retelling of her most recent school drama. At ten, everything was a scandal. Luckily for Robyn, Fiadh didn't require much response. She was happy to have an audience. Plus, now that Lexi had returned, Fiadh's focus was back on her new idol.

Lexi was a hit tonight, and not just with her niece. The difference in her mother was noticeable from the minute they'd walked in and she'd seen Robyn and Lexi standing together. Robyn had been surprised when Lexi's arm moved around her, but the surprise had turned to gratitude when her mom spoke about how happy they looked. Lexi was playing the part very well. So well, in fact, Robyn had a hard time remembering it was an act to begin with. Over the past couple of hours, the light touches and caresses had become more frequent between them. It was strange to experience in real time how naturally they fell into the rhythm.

Fiadh got up to join the other kids who were huddled around an iPad watching something, and Robyn's sister April slid in across from them at their table. April's eyes were on her, and she had a questioning look on her face. Robyn bit her lip, waiting for the inevitable grilling. Her mother was happy to accept Robyn and Lexi's newfound relationship with little question, but they wouldn't get off that lightly with April. Ava missed the middle child syndrome, but April was the epitome of the baby of the family. Spoiled. She was outgoing, mischievous, and loved that she could do no wrong in their mother's eyes. She also had to always know everything and wouldn't let up until she had the latest family gossip. She had a good heart, but Robyn often joked about how it was hidden under a layer of sass.

"So…when did this all happen?"

April pointed a finger between Robyn and Lexi. Robyn squeezed Lexi's fingers where they rested in her palm and suddenly wished they had prepared something. As the silence stretched a little too long and April's brow furrowed quizzically, Robyn realised she needed to come up with something quick.

"What's it been, three months now?"

Robyn turned to look at Lexi and smiled, hoping she'd take the hint. Lexi was the creative one, who consumed a lot of sappy movies and romance books. She would be far better at this than Robyn. Her own go-to genres were crime, mysteries, and thrillers, and she was certain that would be the wrong route to go down.

"Since we officially started dating, or since you started trying to woo me?"

Lexi grinned as Robyn rolled her eyes. Clearly, Lexi was going to have some fun with this.

"Wooing? My sister, really? I didn't think she knew what that looked like."

Robyn scowled at April as Lexi laughed.

"Your sister can be very romantic. Sweet, caring…how could I resist?"

April cocked her head, a sceptical look on her face.

"Okay, now I know you're screwing with me. Sweet and caring is Ava's gig. Robyn is the grumpy, stoic one."

Robyn gripped Lexi's thigh under the table. She had meant it as a quick warning signal, a way to tell her to lay off the theatrics without April seeing. But with the way Lexi's dress rose as she sat, Robyn's fingers pressed into the warm skin above her knee and her stomach flipped. She would have little excuse for leaving her hand where it was, considering nobody was paying attention to what they were doing beneath the oak surface. But suddenly, removing it was the worst idea. Lexi made the decision for her as she slid her hand on top of Robyn's and held it in place.

"Your sister is full of surprises. She has far more sides

than most people seem to see. Myself included, until suddenly it was all I could see."

Robyn gulped at Lexi's statement and tried to remind herself it was just a story.

"Like last weekend, she surprised me with an early morning trip to cheer me up."

The skin of Robyn's palm prickled with heat where it lay on Lexi's thigh. Lexi's thumb was making soft circles on her hand absentmindedly as she spoke, and it was driving Robyn to distraction. She tried to summon words to steer the conversation onto safer topics but the light touch of Lexi's fingers was taking most of her focus. A thought that had Robyn wondering how those fingers would feel on so many other areas of her body.

The heat rose up her face. She hoped that her sister would take that as embarrassment due to Lexi's more embellished and romantic version of their morning at the car boot sale. The funny thing was, none of it was really a lie. Sure, Lexi exaggerated some of the details, adding more implied meaning than there had been. But the facts remained the same.

"That was really sweet, Robs. Thoughtful. Seems like you got more from Dad than just his looks."

Robyn smiled and her heart squeezed at the mention of her father. Although Robyn was twelve when he died, she could still easily recall how in love her parents were. Her dad made it hard not to notice. He would come home with flowers, not just on special occasions, but regularly. He would often tell them how lucky he was that their mom chose him and how he would make sure she never regretted it. He always said how he wanted to make sure his girls grew up seeing how they should be treated by a man, so they'd never accept any less. His wish had come true with his youngest daughters at least. Both their husbands were the kind of men her father would have approved of. Technically, his wish had come true for Robyn, too. She wouldn't accept any less from a man, considering she had no interest in men romantically.

"Hey, somebody's gotta keep up the family legacy of sweet-talking women. The sacrifices I make."

"Woman. Not women. If you want to live up to your father, you need to stick to one this time."

Robyn heard her mother before she saw her. How long had she been behind them, listening? She came and joined their table as Robyn deflated. They were back to this already? She hoped this fake relationship would get her at least one night without criticism.

"Yes, Mom, I know. You've mentioned that a time or two."

To her surprise, her mom reached out her hand and grasped Robyn's where it lay on the table. Her other one was still firmly planted on Lexi's thigh, and she was suddenly grateful for the grounded feeling it provided as she schooled her features. The last thing she wanted was to make it obvious that it was a big deal, but the truth was it had been longer than she cared to remember since her mom held her hand like this.

"It's obvious seeing you two together that I don't need to worry about that anymore. You've found *do chroí.*"

Hearing her mother speak the words in Irish brought back so many memories for Robyn. That's what her dad used to call her mom. *Mo chroí.* My heart. They heard him say it so often that it came to mean *love* to her and her sisters. She could practically hear her father's voice in her ears, reminding her of what was most important. *Find your love.* Love and family were the most important things. Love and family were her father's heart, and his wish for them.

All eyes were on Robyn as she turned her head to look at Lexi. The promise which led her mother to speak the words might be a lie, the relationship fake, but hearing them filled Robyn's heart regardless. She was so grateful to Lexi. She was grateful for tonight, for Lexi giving Robyn the chance to enjoy this time with her family. Even if it was only a mirage of what life could be. She was grateful for the way Lexi charmed everyone around her into believing their fake love was real and so damn wonderful. And mostly, she was grateful for the person who had brought happiness and silliness and fun to her life for the past few years.

Right then, while Lexi's hand still covered hers on her thigh, Robyn couldn't pretend that the fake relationship was only for her family's benefit. All she knew, all she could think or feel, was that she had never wanted to kiss someone so much in her whole life. She leaned in, pausing a fraction away from Lexi's mouth. When Lexi's eyes closed in anticipation, she closed the gap and kissed the lips that were just as soft as they looked.

❖

Lexi kept her eyes closed for a beat even after Robyn's lips left hers. She opened them to see Robyn's face already turned back, fielding more questions about their new love from her mom and sisters. Lexi reached up and ran a finger over her own bottom lip distractedly.

Did that really happen?

The tingling of her mouth told her that yes it had. She glanced to the side and saw April's eyes on her, a broad smile across her face. She must look like the picture of lovestruck— gazing dreamily at her girlfriend and savouring their brief kiss. Because that's what it had been, a brief, chaste kiss that Robyn likely initiated to prove her mother's words true. Robyn didn't intend the effect it was currently having on Lexi, but it was happening all the same.

Lexi excused herself to go to the bathroom. The skin of her thigh prickled, missing the warmth of Robyn's touch already. The bathroom was small, only two stalls, and luckily both were vacant. Lexi stood in front of the ornate gold mirror that stretched across the double sink and stared at her reflection. She looked normal on the outside. Her lips, still burning with the memory of Robyn's, didn't retain a mark, bar a little less gloss. She took the tube of lip gloss from her purse and reapplied it.

The door to the bathroom opened and part of Lexi longed for it to be Robyn, coming to check on her. When April walked through behind her, disappointment mingled with a hint of relief, coursed through her. Lexi wasn't sure, within the small confines of the bathroom and after the confusing moment they'd had, that she would be able to resist complicating things more if Robyn stood before her right now.

"It's good seeing you two together. My sister looks happier than I've seen in a long time."

Lexi smiled at April, who had joined her at the sink.

"I always assumed she'd continue her love 'em and leave 'em ways, well, without the loving part. And here you've got her shacking up already. The roommate part could get really awkward if things went south."

Lexi bristled at April's words and the laughter that followed. April caught sight of her face in the mirror and grimaced.

"Sorry, that sounded worse than I intended. Shit, I didn't mean anything bad. I love Robyn. She's always been an amazing big sister. I just know how much it hurt her losing Dad, and I've heard her talk so many times about relationships being a road back to that pain that she didn't want to travel. I'm glad she changed her mind for you. You're good for her. Don't let my big mouth scare you off."

April shot an apologetic smile and Lexi let her off the hook. Not only because she was accustomed to inserting her foot in her mouth and knew what it was like, but because she owed April. After hearing all of that, it was a lot easier for Lexi to snap back to reality and remember that this was all an act, and Robyn was not in fact here to woo Lexi in real life.

"You're good. If your sister's snoring hasn't scared me off yet, your big mouth has no chance."

April smiled at her and squeezed her arm softly before excusing herself to one of the stalls. Lexi headed back to the table and slid into her seat again, ready to continue the night as planned. And the plan had been to give Robyn a night to enjoy time with her family, not to complicate the real friendship they shared. April might have spoken out of turn, but her words were the only truth of the evening. *The roommate part could get really awkward if things went south.*

Robyn moved her hand, and it hovered above Lexi's briefly. Lexi pretended not to notice, turning her head to talk to April's husband Luke. She didn't want to make it awkward and reject Robyn's contact, but right now she didn't feel like encouraging it either. When the contact never came, Lexi had a twinge of regret. But she needed to keep perspective and April had given her that.

Robyn wasn't the relationship type. Lexi knew that better than anyone. Women came and went from their apartment through the years and rarely the same one twice in a row. They were roommates. It wasn't like a one-night stand was really an option on their table. Was that what Lexi wanted? Was Robyn even attracted to her? Lexi hadn't been secretly pining for Robyn all this time. Sure, lately things had been happening around Robyn. Feelings she wasn't quite sure how to place. But nothing concrete, nothing she would pin down and say yes, this was obvious. But that kiss, as brief as it was, opened a floodgate in Lexi's mind with all these unexplored territories that hadn't been present before.

Heat flushed through her body at the idea of a night with Robyn. Lexi hadn't ever been a one-night stand kind of person. She likely never would be. But feelings like this didn't happen often for her, and she was reluctant to ignore them completely. As Robyn touched her arm lightly, Lexi jumped a little and turned to face her, hoping that the salacious images running through her mind weren't obvious on her face. Robyn removed her hand quickly.

"Sorry, I was just saying we should head out soon. It's getting late."

Lexi tuned back into the room around her. It had dwindled down to a handful of people—most of the extended family were gone. Robyn's immediate family remained and were all in lively conversation with one another. Lexi wasn't sure how long she had been zoned out, wandering down the rabbit hole where her lustful daydreams had taken her.

"Are you okay?"

Concern was etched along Robyn's brow, and Lexi connected her brain back to her mouth to set her at ease.

"Yeah, yes, I'm good. I've had a great night."

She plastered what she hoped was a reassuring smile on her face and stood. Robyn still didn't look convinced. She leaned in close, and something deep inside Lexi shivered at the feel of Robyn's breath tickling her ear.

"I'm sorry. The kiss was probably too far. I should've checked with you first."

Robyn's voice was low because they were standing very close to her family. Lexi reached out and linked their fingers together. She smiled up at eyes so dark they were almost black in the dim lighting. Rather than reaching up and pulling Robyn's lips back against her own like she wanted to, Lexi leaned up on her tiptoes and brushed her lips softly across Robyn's cheek. She raised her voice loud enough so Robyn's mother, who was eyeing them up nearby, could hear.

"Let's go, baby."

Robyn's cheeks pinked up in an adorable fashion and Lexi turned to the onlookers, not letting go of her grip on Robyn's hand.

"Thanks for inviting me tonight. It was great. I loved getting to celebrate with you all."

She smiled genuinely at the chorus of goodbyes. Marie walked them out, all the while talking about how she couldn't wait to see them again and making plans with Robyn to get lunch together. Robyn's grip got tighter in hers at every word. This must be hard for her. Bittersweet, even.

Despite the confusion racing around her body and the possible awkwardness that could ensue, Lexi couldn't bring herself to regret the evening. Not with the look that had appeared on Robyn's face as her mother hugged them both before they got into the awaiting taxi. Not with the hand still clasped in hers the whole car journey home.

And certainly not with the memory of Robyn's lips on hers as she lay in bed that night, repaying her body for the months of neglect she'd shown herself.

CHAPTER EIGHT

Robyn hadn't driven to work that Monday morning. Her plan had been to grab a few drinks after shift and see where the night took her. Most of the time it took her into someone else's bed, or brought someone else into hers, so not having to worry about collecting her car the next morning was preferable. She took a short walk down to Blaze, the one queer bar in the area. It always made her chuckle seeing the flames emblazoned on the sign out front. Fire, flames, heat…clearly, she couldn't get enough in or out of work.

She walked in and nodded to a few familiar faces. Her eyes landed on a brunette who was currently engrossed in a game of pool. She looked vaguely familiar, but Robyn was sure she hadn't seen her in the bar before. In a city as small as theirs, it was rare to see a completely new face in a place like this, especially on a quiet Monday night. But Blaze was more than simply a place to get drunk and dance the night away. It had old-school arcade machines as well as the pool tables, and it served food until nine p.m. It drew a steady crowd both day and night.

Robyn usually had no difficulty finding someone else out looking for uncomplicated orgasms, even midweek. She ordered a drink and her eyes flickered back to the brunette again. The woman was beautiful, but Robyn found that the usual spark of excitement at the prospect of making her way over to introduce herself was missing. As Robyn scanned the rest of the room, she smiled toward the redhead seated at a table beside the dance floor who waved her over.

"Hey, Robbie. I haven't seen you here in a while."

Robyn shrugged and took a sip of her drink before eyeing up her companion. Something was different.

"I could say the same to you, Dani. You disappeared for a while, I figured Ruby finally got her shit together and took you off the market."

Dani laughed across from her, her eyes sparkling. *Got it in one.*

"Yeah, Ruby was back in town for a little while between jobs. We spent some time together, but she's moved away for work now."

Robyn winced in sympathy. "Shit, that sucks. I'm sorry."

Dani shrugged with a forced lightness that didn't quite match her face.

"She's in sales and got offered a hard-to-refuse contract in Edinburgh. I mourned with a lot of ice cream for a while. My friend Ollie"—Dani nodded toward the brunette who had caught Robyn's eye—"moved to the city not that long ago and wanted to check out the *queer scene.*"

She put air quotes around the last two words and they both laughed. The queer scene in their city was basically this bar, so there wasn't a whole lot to check out.

"I figured I'd finally show my face before people started sending search parties. It's strange, when you're single for so long, you get used to seeing the same faces most weekends. It becomes an unwritten expectation."

Robyn nodded her agreement. "Yeah, I noticed your friend when I walked in right away, because as you said, you get used to seeing the usuals."

Dani picked up her drink and took a sip. "She's getting over her own broken heart, so she's come here alone the past couple of weeks before she convinced me to get out of my slump and come out with her. She was disappointed when I pointed out that she'd already explored the extent of the queer scene, but I tagged along tonight anyway. I'm surprised you didn't bump into each other before now."

Dani's face gave away more than her politely worded sentence did.

"You mean you're surprised we haven't slept together?"

Dani shrugged, and Robyn didn't blame her for the thought. Ollie was her type and Robyn had set a precedent for herself the past few years. One she wasn't quite sure she wanted to live up to anymore. She hadn't realised how little she'd gone out recently. It hadn't been a conscious decision. She hadn't been in the mood for where the night would inevitably lead. Before, knowing she would end the night with someone was the excitement of coming out. Now, it was more of a deterrent.

Spending the last couple of weekends with Lexi had been a different kind of excitement. A feeling that kept the loneliness at bay and filled her heart at the thought of spending more time with Lexi.

"Where'd you go just now? Wow…did you meet someone? Like, someone who is an actual *someone*?"

Robyn rolled her eyes as heat crept up her neck.

"That sentence doesn't even make sense, Dani. Everyone is someone."

Dani's eyes crinkled at the sides, a knowing look on her face. "You keep telling yourself that, Robbie. How's Lexi? I haven't heard from her in a while."

Dani was an artist and had become somewhat of a mentor for Lexi when she was starting out with her career. If the queer community in their small city was tight-knit, the art community was even more so. And the overlap between the two was significant. Which should've made Lexi's *I never said I was straight* revelation less of a surprise.

"She's...okay. I'd say she could use an artistic shoulder to lean on right about now if you've got the time to reach out to her."

Dani nodded and took a sip of her drink before replying.

"She's lucky to have you looking out for her. Especially with Sam and Brooke busy with baby prep. I'll give her a call."

Part of Robyn wanted to spill the thoughts racing around her head to Dani. To let out the confusing feelings she was having that were making themselves far more noticeable since learning that Lexi was not straight. Those feelings became harder again after the kiss they'd shared two days prior. That memory kept popping up in her mind every time she closed her eyes. But even if she was inclined to open up about it, Dani wasn't the person to do it with.

Dani was far more Lexi's person than she was Robyn's. Aside from the mentoring, she was best friends with Lexi's sister-in-law, Brooke. Sharing her feelings and her dilemma about Lexi with Dani would make a complicated situation even more complex.

"Anyway, tell me more about what happened with Ruby. Why did she go? Hell, why didn't you?"

Dani took a sip of her drink as her eyebrows pulled downward.

"Her work is important to her. She wanted to go. The work I'm doing with the centre had just gone to a whole new level with the funding we got, and I couldn't just walk away from that. It was bad timing."

Dani shrugged, but she was clearly more broken up than she would admit. Having seen Dani and Ruby together, Robyn had always guessed they would eventually work out their feelings for each other. Ollie bounded over to their table before Robyn could reply, a crinkle forming between her eyebrows as she turned to greet Robyn.

"Hey! Have we met before?"

That niggling in Robyn's head that she knew Ollie intensified at the question.

"I don't know. I did think you looked familiar, but I can't place where from. Dani says you're new in town? I'm Robyn, by the way."

Ollie nodded and shot her a smile, the crinkle between her eyes still present, before turning her attention to Dani.

"I just came over to check on you before I kick more ass at pool. You sure you don't want to play?"

"No, I'm good, I'm actually going to head out. I'm not feeling it tonight. You sticking around to see where the night leads?"

"I'll come with you. Let me grab my stuff."

Dani shook her head before Ollie had a chance to move, as Robyn watched the back and forth.

"No, honestly, you stay and enjoy the night. I promise I'm okay. I'll only feel guilty if you leave."

Eventually reassured, Ollie headed back to play pool with a quick wave to Robyn. Dani got up to leave, her shoulders heavier than before. Robyn regretted pushing about Ruby and wondered if that lead to the early departure.

"I'm sorry, Dani, I shouldn't have poked at the clearly still fresh wound. I didn't mean to throw your night off."

Dani shook her head as she put on her coat.

"You didn't, honestly. I came, I saw, I realized I'm not quite ready. And that's okay. Plus, I should get out of here before the blonde goddess walking our way pounces on you."

Dani winked and smiled as Robyn swivelled her head around to see who Dani was referring to.

"Hey, Robyn. Long time no see. Are you...leaving together?"

Freya glanced between her and Dani before focusing her attention back on Robyn. Robyn hesitated a moment, taking in the look Freya gave her. It would be so easy to stay here with Freya, have a drink and wind up back in bed together. Robyn rarely spent two nights with someone, but Freya wasn't the type to read into it anyway. They had worked well together.

"Oh no, I'm—"

"Yeah, I'm heading home. Good to see you again, Freya, enjoy your night."

Robyn got up to leave too, suddenly not very interested in seeing where else the night would lead. She was surprised to find there was no part of her that regretted the words as they left her lips. Freya smiled and shrugged, heading off in search of someone else to pass the time with.

Robyn and Dani walked outside together, a light breeze moving past them as Robyn debated in her head between calling a taxi or making the thirty-minute walk home. She turned to see Dani looking at her curiously.

"I'm here if you need to discuss anything, Robyn. I know we don't talk much outside of the confines of this bar, but Lexi has my number. Ask her for it if you need to get anything off your chest. Lexi also happens to be a great listener, which I've found out first-hand, so I'm sure she could help with whatever you've got going on too."

Robyn's face flushed at the mention of Lexi, and she quickly ducked her head into her bag to grab her phone under the pretence of ordering that taxi. As she glanced back up, Dani was sporting a slight knowing smile and nodded her head.

"Aha. Understood. Well, good luck, and the offer stands."

Before Robyn could ask what she meant by the proclamation, Dani turned and walked away. Robyn watched her go for a moment under the streetlamps that lit the darkening night. She was left feeling a little like she'd had some sort of weird fever dream that she was waiting to wake up from. *Dani understood.* What did that mean for Robyn? Because right now, she felt like she barely understood it herself.

❖

Lexi was sprawled on the floor, still catching her breath after a game of tag with her adorable, but far too fast, nephew. Finley had been carted off to bed by Sam while Brooke sat on the couch, an amused expression on her face.

"So…she kissed you, and you don't know if she likes you? Listen, Lex, I know you said you're not a lesbian, but you sure as hell sound like one right about now."

Lexi rolled her eyes and pulled herself up to sit cross legged on the floor facing Brooke.

"That's not exactly what I said. I told you about the whole fake date thing. She kissed me because it was part of the act."

Brooke's face screamed sceptical, and Lexi could tell she was trying her best to hide a smile.

"Sorry, kiddo. But that sounds like a little more than the script called for. What kinda kiss was it anyway? Was there tongue?"

Brooke wiggled her eyebrows as Sam returned from bedtime duty.

"Whose tongue? Do I want to hear this?"

Sam threw herself down next to her wife and linked her fingers through Brooke's. The sweet smile she threw Brooke's way made Lexi's heart melt. Three years on and they were still couple goals.

"Oh, you most definitely do. Your sister has got a crush on her roommate."

Sam gave Lexi a wide-eyed look and Lexi groaned, letting her face fall into her hands.

"That's *definitely* not what I said. You need to get those pregnancy hormones under control."

Brooke launched a cushion at her, which was well deserved. It wasn't Brooke's fault that Lexi had spewed everything out in a rambling mess simply because Brooke asked how she was. But if there was anyone that would get it, it was Brooke. Sam sat forward in the chair, giving Lexi her attention.

"You want to tell me what you actually said? I mean, I've seen Robyn, so I don't blame you. But I feel like I've missed something vital, since we talked not all that long ago, and you've never mentioned being attracted to…well, anyone."

Lexi knew what Sam was getting at. She had never mentioned to her lesbian sister that she was attracted to women. Yes, she'd opened up to her about her demisexuality, but she didn't specify anything about gender. It was probably a little bizarre for Sam to hear about the possibility of that like this.

Lexi shrugged, trying to find words to convey all the feelings bubbling inside.

"I know. Did I know being attracted to women was a possibility? Yeah, sure. I wasn't purposefully hiding it from anyone, it just wasn't something I really thought too much about since there wasn't a reason to at the time."

Brooke spoke then and her voice was kind, but firm.

"You don't need to explain yourself to us, or anyone. Everyone has their own path to figuring themselves out and you don't ever have to rush along that path for anyone else. Nobody is entitled to pieces of you that you're not ready to give. I'm glad you wanted to share that with us, but if anyone makes assumptions about your sexuality, that's on them. Not you. Okay?"

Brooke was the best at jumping into protective, mothering mode. Lexi smiled widely at her.

"That kiddo upstairs and that kiddo in there are so lucky to have you both as moms, you know that?"

Sam plopped herself on the floor next to Lexi and pulled her in for a quick hug. Brooke discreetly wiped a stray tear from her eye.

"Stop. Pregnancy hormones can't handle compliments."

Lexi laughed as Sam hopped back up onto the couch. She moved herself to the single recliner next to them and settled in. Lexi loved evenings like this, with nowhere to be and nothing to do but enjoy the company of her family.

"Stop trying to make us all mushy just to change the subject. I want details. I heard something about tongue, and that does not seem like lack of attraction territory to me."

Lexi thought back to the kiss. It was far more PG than they were thinking, but there was no doubt about attraction playing a part, for Lexi at least.

"No tongue, I'm afraid."

Sam exaggerated a pout and Brooke rolled her eyes, making Lexi chuckle. The laughter eased the tension that coiled inside her at the thought of laying it all out there. So that's what she did. She started before the car boot sale, explaining everything about the commissions, and Robyn's kind gestures, and their fake date. She left out the pleasuring herself to the memory of the kiss part, but she was sure they could fill in the blanks on that. She explained about Robyn's reputation, and what April had said, and her hesitance at ruining their current situation warring with not wanting to lose this feeling.

"So let me clarify. You sobbed into her hoodie, so her response was to organize a unique first, I mean *friend*, date to a place you love to go. She carried your bags along the way. You offered to go to her sister's anniversary as her date. The thought of Robyn being with other women right now makes your face look like you sucked on a lemon. She kissed you and it made your knees all weak. And you're unsure about... what exactly?"

When Sam laid it all out like that, it made Lexi wonder what exactly had her so unsure too. Then she remembered what April had said and bit her lip as she parroted the sentiment.

"She's my roommate. Has been for almost four years now and it's worked well. She's not just my roommate, she's one of the most important people in my life. Is that really worth risking?"

She sat waiting for either of them to speak as they glanced at each other, utilizing that secret couple way they had of talking without words. She watched the small smile that grew on Sam's face as she turned her attention back to Lexi.

"Look who you're asking, Lex. We're living proof that it is."

CHAPTER NINE

I've barely seen you this week. You avoiding me, Robbie?"

Robyn rolled her eyes at Lexi as she threw her bag down and flopped onto the couch. Lexi sat beside her, and Robyn sank into the cushions. She was exhausted after returning from a busy shift.

"If I was avoiding you, I'd just hide in my room like I do when you're dancing to that terrible music you listen to."

A cushion hit Robyn square in the face, and she laughed at the scowl Lexi exaggerated as Robyn placed the weaponized cushion behind her back.

"I worked some extra shifts to cover for one of the guys. His kid just graduated from college and he planned a big celebratory trip for them. You know, before she ventures out into the land of employment where summers off are no longer a thing."

Lexi shrugged, a sheepish smile on her face. "I aim to never experience that first-hand."

Robyn rolled her eyes with a smile before continuing.

"It's adorable, he's the picture of a proud father. He's spent months talking about it, so the rest of the station all pitched in to make sure he got the time off he needed."

"That's sweet of you all. Lucky kid to have so many people looking out for her already," Lexi said.

Robyn nodded at the truth of the statement. Firefighters' kids were treated like family by everyone at the station. She knew that only too well from her own experience. She had grown up with so many aunts and uncles from her dad's team.

Anytime Robyn saw a father get to celebrate these milestones with their kids, it filled her with such conflicting emotions. Happiness that those kids got to experience that type of love and support, and sadness that her time experiencing that with her father was cut so short. She had no doubt he would've offered unwavering support, like he had for the first twelve years of her life. But how would he feel about the way she was living her life now?

"Where'd you go just now?"

Lexi's soft words made Robyn snap back to attention, the memories still flitting before her eyes.

"I was just thinking about my dad."

Lexi nodded, looking at her with a hint of hesitance before speaking. "Can you tell me more about him? If you want to, I'd like to hear it."

Robyn found that the thought didn't terrify her as much as it usually would. Speaking about her father always came with conflicting emotions, and talking about the past in general wasn't her strong suit. But something about the way Lexi looked at her had her pushing all of that aside.

"He loved being a firefighter. He trained hard and worked his way through the ranks quickly. It was a dream of his from childhood."

Declan Moore was the type of man who followed childhood dreams and regarded passion as the highest skill for anything you did in life.

"My mom wasn't as motivated by hopes and dreams as my dad was, but they worked. He always said she kept him grounded, and he loosened her up."

Lexi laughed lightly, laying her head back against the couch and listening intently.

"He loved his job, but he loved us more. I never doubted that. They adored each other in that way those movies you love show. They never seemed to run out of things to talk about. I grew up seeing love not as this big, miraculous thing. But as so many little things. Something I took for granted until suddenly…it was gone."

Robyn found herself flashing to the one day she had never spoken about, not to anyone. She gulped and decided to let the words come out before she lost her nerve.

"One day my dad went to work and never came home. It was a house fire. It started in the kitchen with an unattended frying pan. It only took minutes for the whole kitchen to go up, helped along by a pair of curtains that should never have been hung so close to a cooker. It was a perfect storm of fire hazards."

Robyn saw the concern in Lexi's eyes but was grateful she didn't speak. She sat with Robyn, giving her space to work through the warring thoughts in her mind.

"My Uncle Mikey, he was dad's second in command, was the one who had to break the news. He knocked on the door about an hour before Dad was due home from work. My mom had the dinner on. Corned beef, I remember it so clearly. It was my dad's favourite."

Robyn took a breath, the memories she kept locked up so tightly suddenly crashing to the forefront of her mind. She had been at the table doing homework, complaining about fractions when the knock came at the door. She went to grab it, but her mom beat her to it.

"The minute my mom opened the door to Mikey and saw his hat in his hands, she knew."

Robyn vividly recalled standing in the hallway as her

usually stoic mother fell to the floor, shaking her head and muttering *no*, over and over again. Robyn could still remember the smell of the burnt meat as it sat forgotten on the hob until Robyn herself went and turned it off.

"I still can't eat corned beef." Robyn laughed lightly, hoping to ease the heaviness she had brought to the room.

Lexi moved closer and placed a hand over hers and squeezed lightly. "Good thing I don't like it much, either. We're a corned beef free zone here."

Robyn's smile was more genuine this time as she focused on the weight of Lexi's hand still holding hers.

"I remember April and Ava came running down the stairs when they heard mom yelling. April was asking a million questions. Ava was quiet. I took them into the living room and turned on the TV, putting on a video. I don't even know what I was thinking other than I needed to protect them from what was happening."

They didn't get to watch TV much during a school day. Robyn remembered thinking a cartoon would keep them distracted while she tried to pick up the pieces of her mother from their hallway floor.

"Do you know how many Disney movies start with a parent dying? It wasn't something I paid much attention to until that day."

The images flashed back of standing in the doorway, halfway between the living room and the hall where Mikey was consoling her mother. Her mom had moved from the floor to the stairs as they spoke in hushed tones. As the cartoon animal began to sob for his father to wake up, tears started to flow freely from her eyes. She remembered sliding down the door frame, feeling a little like that cartoon cub. Lost, broken, and like she needed to run away.

Robyn was lost between the then and now, remembering

small arms encircling her as she lifted her head to find Ava pulling her close. Except, right now, it was Lexi's arms that surrounded her. Robyn became aware of the tears wetting her cheeks as Lexi's palm moved in circles on her back.

"I wanted to be brave. For my sisters, for my mom. But mostly because it's what my dad would have done. I guess that's the first time I tried to fill his shoes."

Robyn sniffled and straightened a little, but Lexi continued the soothing movement on her back. Part of her wanted to snatch back all the words and lock them up tight with the memories, but they kept coming.

"You know what the worst part was? Hope. I heard Mikey say he would bring Mom to the hospital and his wife could watch us. I just remember thinking people didn't go to the hospital if they were dead, right? They went there to get better. Maybe Dad was just really hurt. That hope lasted about five seconds until I heard the end of his sentence, *to say goodbye.* I got so mad. Why was I staying at home? I wanted to say goodbye too. He was my dad."

Her voice cracked on the last word, and she took a minute to gather herself. She refused to let any more tears fall. Robyn recalled running out of the room to say that to her mother. She would never forget standing in front of her mom. She would never forget the first time she saw the haunted look on her mom's face when she stared at Robyn, a look she had seen more times than she could count throughout the years. The speed at which her mom averted her gaze startled Robyn so much that she didn't open her mouth. She didn't shout about how unfair it was not to bring them. She didn't say a thing.

"That was the first time I saw that look on my mom's face." Robyn all but whispered.

Lexi waited a beat before speaking in a soft tone. "What look?"

Robyn had locked herself in the bathroom when her mom had left for the hospital. She had stared at her reflection in the small mirror above the sink, studying the deep brown colour of her eyes, the darkness of her hair, even the shape of her face. It had always been a joke growing up that her mom went through days of labour and Robyn was born with ninety percent of her father's genes. It had always been funny, until that moment.

"The way she looked at me like she had seen a ghost."

Robyn would never forget the day her life changed and her idyllic childhood was shattered into a million pieces that used to be made of love. But she hadn't realized until this moment how many details she remembered so clearly. How much she was holding on to in the not so neatly packaged recesses of her mind.

Looking back, it was strange to imagine that her mother was only the age Robyn was now when she was suddenly widowed with three children. The future her parents had worked so hard for and imagined had disappeared. Which was part of the reason Robyn could never understand why her mom of all people still pushed the notion of love and marriage on Robyn, as if it was the most important thing in the world. Why would Robyn want to hang her happiness on something so fragile?

As far as Robyn was concerned, nothing was scarier than loving someone so much that losing them had her broken on the floor, with a future she could no longer control.

"I'm glad you told me this, Robbie. I know it wasn't easy for you. Your dad sounds like an amazing person. So clearly, you got far more than his looks."

With each whispered word Lexi spoke, Robyn pushed past the fear screaming at her to run. Instead, she sank further into Lexi's comforting arms. As she listened to Lexi's heartbeat beneath her and synced her breathing to the rhythm, one loud sentence flitted around in her head.

Maybe Mom has a point.

❖

Lexi was humming to a random pop playlist that she had thrown on for background noise while cleaning the apartment. She had woken up with a lot of energy that morning and no plans, so it was perfect timing for a spring clean. It wasn't even ten yet and she had the bathroom scrubbed, the kitchen gleaming, and she was currently sitting on the living room floor surrounded by stacks of old CDs. She was trying to decide whether to rearrange them by genre or alphabetically when she heard Robyn's bedroom door open.

Getting to comfort Robyn the night before as Robyn opened up to her had felt like a vital moment. However, Lexi couldn't help but wonder if Robyn would have regrets after the emotional evening. By the glare Robyn was currently aiming toward her, though, things were business as usual. Lexi paused her music and tilted her head to the side.

"Something wrong, grumpy?"

Robyn's glare turned to a scowl as she stalked to the kitchen and flicked on the kettle, turning to lean back against the counter. "Why are you and your music so perky at this hour of the morning?"

Lexi grinned. Sweet and caring Robyn was a novelty, and Lexi loved her, but she secretly adored grumpy Robyn.

"It's almost ten a.m. The morning is over. I've been up for hours already, and I got so much cleaning done."

Robyn surveyed the room and looked back at Lexi quizzically.

"Um, Lex, I'm not sure if you know this, but cleaning means things generally look cleaner afterward."

Lexi looked around her, taking in the room through Robyn's eyes. There were CDs placed in what almost resembled piles. A couple of mugs dotted the coffee table because she made herself tea, then forgot about it and made herself another cup. There was a box of photos on the couch with photo albums that she had started sorting through before moving onto the CDs. Then there were the clothes piled over the chair that she had cleared from her closet and planned to bag for charity.

"Okay, I see what this looks like. But it's not like last time. I will finish all these things."

Robyn poured herself tea and nodded along the way you do when you don't believe a word someone is saying.

"Seriously I will. Go look in the bathroom. It's spotless! And see the kitchen, I scrubbed it all before I started on this stuff."

Robyn sipped her tea and ran a finger along the countertop.

"It is very clean. You even got that red wine stain off. That's impressive."

Lexi beamed at the compliment and stood up, grabbing the black bags to start dumping the clothes into.

"See, I told you. Now go check out our very clean bathroom."

"I'm drinking my tea, I'll check—"

Robyn stopped mid-sentence and held her hands up, backing toward the bathroom as Lexi shot her an exaggerated pout. It always worked. She stood in the doorway as Robyn inspected their bathroom. It didn't take long considering the space was tiny, consisting of a toilet, sink and a walk-in shower that took up most of the room. Robyn turned abruptly, obviously not realising Lexi was behind her and came to a halt inches away.

"Whoops, sorry."

Robyn's eyes dropped to her lips quickly and then back up. The temperature increased in the enclosed space as Lexi's throat went dry. They had entered into a staring contest, one that Lexi was reluctant to lose. She pulled her bottom lip between her teeth and bit lightly, watching Robyn's eyes drop back down to follow the action. Lexi's skin tingled at the look that appeared on Robyn's face. She knew she was threading a very fine line, but she couldn't help wanting that look to last.

Robyn stepped closer, so close her loose T-shirt brushed against Lexi's arm where it was crossed in front of her. Lexi dropped her hand and it grazed against Robyn's as it fell. Time stood still as the tension between them became palpable. It was likely only minutes since they had moved from the kitchen, but right now, as she got lost in Robyn's eyes, it could've been hours. Something grazed against her fingers, and her heart started to beat faster. She tried to will her eyes into glancing down and confirming her suspicions—that Robyn was currently stroking her fingers across Lexi's. But she couldn't take her eyes off Robyn's face—she couldn't look away from those eyes.

Robyn's face held so many things it was hard to piece them apart. Hesitance, uncertainty, confusion, and lust. Seeing Robyn on edge because of her made Lexi feel things she would never have expected. She felt confident, playful, and in control. Part of her wanted to see how far she could push Robyn before her usually cool exterior cracked. Robyn inhaled pointedly and leaned a little closer. Lexi wondered if she was going to kiss her. It didn't terrify her as much as it excited her.

Robyn pivoted her head toward Lexi's ear at the last minute and whispered, "You planning to stand there all day or are you going to let me pass?"

The light scent of smoke that always clung to Robyn's

hair after a late shift mingled with the stronger smell of lemon air freshener she had used in the bathroom. She waited a beat before answering and noticed Robyn's hand was shaking slightly beside her own.

"I guess I'll move. But only after you lavish me with praise for my cleaning." She grinned as Robyn closed her eyes briefly and took a deeper, slow breath, dramatizing her exasperation. Then Lexi followed up her statement with one that would push her right over that line she had been pretending not to cross. "Is it such a hardship being forced to stand here and worship me?"

Robyn's eyes widened and Lexi's stomach flipped at the near growl from Robyn. Her innuendo wasn't lost on Robyn, it seemed, because she flushed bright red and looked away. Lexi was having far too much fun to stop and consider what the hell she was doing, or how far she was willing to go with this. When Robyn looked back at her, any doubt she had about whether Robyn was attracted to her disappeared.

Suddenly, something shifted in Robyn's face, and the change sent shivers through Lexi. Robyn's gaze roamed up and down Lexi's body and Lexi felt herself respond in an unfamiliar, but not unwelcome, way.

"I am *more* than happy to worship you, Sunny. The bathroom is beautiful. So nice, in fact, I think I'll skip breakfast and shower."

Robyn took a couple of precise steps back before continuing. "Maybe we can eat together when I'm done."

She pulled her T-shirt over her head as Lexi watched, mouth agape. Robyn was sporting a string top underneath, which should've slowed down Lexi's heart rate. Except the way the thin, cotton material clung to Robyn, who was undoubtedly braless, was somehow sexier than what Lexi had imagined. How had she become the mouse and Robyn the cat in their impromptu game?

Robyn hooked her thumbs into the waistband of her pants and teased her. "You gonna stand and watch? Either way, mind closing the door?"

Lexi shook herself and backed slowly out of the room, not taking her eyes off Robyn until the last moment. She mumbled something about starting breakfast as she shut the bathroom door and turned to lean against it. Lexi was the one who had started the game, and somehow, Robyn had still beaten her at it.

CHAPTER TEN

R obyn stood in the shower with her hands flat against the cold tiled wall. Hot water cascaded down her body and one word reverberated through her head. *Shit*. She took some deep breaths, ignoring the ache between her legs as she tried to pull herself together. What in the hell had just happened?

Lexi had been flirting with her. That much was clear. She could stand in here and worry about if she'd interpreted it wrong or if she was hearing what she wanted to hear, but that would be self-deception. There was absolutely no doubt in Robyn's mind that her sweet, kind, bubbly roommate had attempted, and succeeded, in teasing Robyn in a way she never would've imagined Lexi capable of. Not only that—she had looked at Robyn like she wanted to devour her where she stood.

Robyn's knees almost buckled at the vivid images that thought conjured. A part of her was kicking herself for not dragging Lexi into this shower with her to allow her to do just that. But the way Lexi's demeanour had shifted from confident and playful to quiet and hesitant when Robyn had taken over their little back-and-forth made her think it wouldn't have been the right move.

When they were pressed so close together she could feel Lexi's breath against her, Robyn had a choice to make. She could've inched forward instead of back and pressed her lips to

Lexi's. She could picture exactly how that would have played out. Lexi's arms would have come up to wrap around her neck, pulling Robyn's lips more firmly against hers. Robyn would have wrapped her own arms around Lexi's waist and pulled her closer, their lips melding in the way they had only hinted at with the previous, far too chaste, kiss.

Robyn had taken the far less exciting and safer route. She had stepped back, thrown in a little teasing of her own to make it clear to Lexi that the situation wasn't unwelcome, and given Lexi the opportunity to take her own step back if she needed to. The partial undressing was probably uncalled for, but the almost comical open-mouthed look it brought to Lexi's face had been worth it. Her libido wasn't thanking her for it, but Lexi wasn't a one-night stand kind of person. She was far too important to Robyn to risk ruining their friendship for a one-night, or morning, passion-fuelled fling.

Robyn switched off the shower and quickly dried herself. She grabbed her robe that hung at the back of the door and slipped into it. Although walking through the living room to her bedroom in a towel was kind of tempting, she needed to try to regroup and figure out what this all meant. It would be far easier to do that in fresh clothes. Robyn needn't have worried anyway because Lexi purposefully stayed facing whatever she had cooking in the frying pan as Robyn made her way to her room and threw on her lounge pants and T-shirt. After a few more deep breaths, she ventured out, mainly because her stomach demanded it.

The smell of bacon made Robyn's stomach rumble as she joined Lexi in the kitchen. Lexi had distracted herself with cooking, by the looks of things. The bacon was joined by sausages, fried eggs, pudding, and toast on two plates ready to go.

"Can you grab the juice?"

These were the first words Lexi had uttered to Robyn since she'd come out of the bathroom, and she said them as nonchalantly as if their earlier encounter had never happened. Robyn grabbed two glasses of orange juice and joined Lexi at their small two-seater table. If Lexi wanted to pretend this morning hadn't happened, maybe that was for the best. It would give Robyn time to get her thoughts together and figure out how she wanted to approach this, if at all. It would give them time to get back into a groove of being roommates and friends.

Robyn had a couple of days off now after her busy work week, so they could find their footing again. She began to relax back at the thought as she chewed slowly, her shoulders dropping with the release of pent-up tension.

"So, nice shower? Did you use all the hot water, or did you need it cold?"

Robyn paused chewing, not wanting to choke on her food as her eyes shot up to Lexi's sparkling ones. She shook her head at the smug look on Lexi's face, clearly proud of herself for having regained the upper hand in this back-and-forth. So many answers sat on the tip of Robyn's tongue to continue the teasing. The mischievous look that Lexi sported made it difficult not to want to keep up the banter. So why did Robyn feel the need to be mature and address things head-on all of a sudden?

"What are we doing, Lex? You're flirting with me. *We're* flirting." Robyn pointed her fork between them to emphasise her point.

Lexi nodded, her face not wavering at the words. "Yup. Good detective skills there, Robbie."

Since when had Lexi gotten a bucket load of sass? They had always been partial to good-natured jibing, but it sounded very different layered with these innuendos.

"We gonna talk about it or were you just planning to pretend it's a normal everyday occurrence?"

Lexi shrugged, finishing the food in her mouth before replying.

"It wasn't exactly a plan at all. I didn't wake up this morning and think maybe I'll flirt with Robyn today. It just happened, and now I can't seem to switch it off. And I kind of don't want to, it's fun."

Robyn was a little taken aback by Lexi's honesty. She wasn't sure anyone had ever been so up front about their intent to flirt with her before. Usually, her interactions with women fell into one of two categories. Category one was made up of subtle flirting and light touches that would build up over an evening, leading to them ending up in bed together. That type took place without much discussion at all. Or category two, her companion for the night would make her intentions very clear from the outset, without much flirting or effort involved on either side.

The latter ended up being more straightforward. Before Robyn had gotten good at setting her own boundaries, category one had often led to assumptions that one night would lead to more. This was something Robyn never entertained. But this time, here with Lexi, was different. Lexi wasn't saying she was trying to get Robyn into bed. She wasn't pretending the flirting wasn't happening. She came right out and said what she meant. And Robyn didn't know how to react.

"Flirting usually has a purpose, in my experience," Robyn said.

Lexi seemed to consider the statement.

"Maybe the purpose is to have fun? I don't know, Robbie. I know it's probably not that simple and I know we have more to consider. But it's the weekend, and I'm finally feeling a little like myself again, and I don't want to be all mature and discuss things. So maybe today can just be a day off from our regularly scheduled adulting?"

Robyn couldn't help laughing at Lexi. She really did seem back to her sunshiney self today, and the last thing Robyn wanted was to derail that. If she had to endure a little flirting to help out, well, that was a sacrifice she was willing to make.

❖

The rest of the morning passed quite quickly. After their late breakfast together and the conversation that ensued, Lexi wondered if things would be weird between them. But they quickly fell back into an easy rhythm. It was almost the same as usual, but with an extra zing to their interactions. That was the only way Lexi could think to describe it.

Around lunchtime, Lexi had most of the place back to normal and flopped onto the couch next to Robyn. Robyn lowered the book she had been reading for the past hour and surveyed Lexi.

"You realise that for someone who wanted a non-adulting day, you did a lot of adulting?"

"Cleaning is only adulting when someone expects me do it," Lexi replied.

Robyn shook her head with a laugh and raised her book back up. Lexi sat for a moment taking in the room, happy with everything she had gotten done so far. Part of her wanted to join Robyn and get lost in a good book, because she looked so relaxed. But Lexi's skin prickled, and her fingers danced along her legs. Trying to focus on a book was pointless when she was this antsy. There was one thing that had always been guaranteed to calm her restless body and mind—but picking up a paintbrush was still terrifying.

The tick-tock of the deadline for her commission wasn't

quite as loud in her head as before, but it was still there. Her eyes landed on the easel still set up in the corner, marred by the messy red and black X from her last failed attempt. Unexpectedly, her head started to fill with ideas. She pictured the lighter colours that could surround the X, marking the spot as a dark contrast to the brightness. She bit her lip as hope blossomed in her chest, while fear rooted her feet to the ground. What if she moved and it all stopped again? What if she picked up the paintbrush and everything disappeared?

"What's going on over there? By your facial expressions, you appear to be having a one-woman argument."

Lexi hadn't realised Robyn was watching her. She toyed with what to say, but the truth had done her well so far today.

"I feel like I want to paint and I have ideas, but I'm afraid if I move I'll lose it all again and end up disappointed."

Robyn sat up a little straighter but didn't move closer. Lexi felt like a stray cat Robyn was afraid to spook.

"Well…you'll also be disappointed if you let this feeling pass without even trying, right?"

She had a point. Lexi nodded and got up before she could think twice. She walked toward the easel and started pouring her paint, mixing the colours until they became the exact shades she envisioned. She glanced to the side and Robyn quickly looked back down at her book. The now-familiar zing flitted across her body at the idea that Robyn was watching her and trying not to get caught. Lexi thought maybe the pressure of having an audience, even a silent one who was pretending to read, would overwhelm her. But as she began to put paintbrush to canvas and see her ideas come to life, she realised it was doing the exact opposite.

Every time she paused, and a little worry crept back in, she would glance at Robyn. At the beginning, she'd seen Robyn's head duck back to her book again. After a while, though, Robyn openly watched her paint, and Lexi found it bolstered her. This piece wouldn't work for the commission she needed to do, but right now it didn't matter. She was painting, creating, doing the thing she loved, and it felt so good. She stood back and took in the piece, touched up a little here and there, and then set the paintbrush down.

As she glanced at the clock she was shocked to find it was past dinnertime. She turned to see that the spot where Robyn had spent most of the day was now vacant. She glanced around the room but couldn't see Robyn. How long had she been gone? The door opened a moment later and Robyn walked through holding bags of Chinese food.

"I figured you'd need sustenance once you were done."

Robyn figured right if Lexi's growling stomach was anything to go by.

"You're the best, now hand it over."

Robyn laughed and held the food back as Lexi made grabby hands toward it.

"Still in immature mode, I see. Grab plates, you're not eating from the bag. I do have limits."

"Oh, do you now?"

Lexi purposefully drew out the sentence and wagged her eyebrows, laughing at Robyn's reddening cheeks. It was a little addictive being able to get Robyn worked up like this. They plated the food, and they sat together on the couch.

"I don't get how you do that," Robyn said.

Lexi took a break from inhaling her food to answer. "What? Eat half my food in a minute?"

Lexi followed Robyn's fork as she pointed it toward the now completed canvas.

"That. I mean, it was a mess earlier. You basically took an angry scribble and made it this amazing thing. It's not even like you just totally painted over it. You transformed it. You took this dark thing and made it so beautiful. I don't understand how you do that."

Lexi's heart squeezed at the sincerity in the words. She looked at the canvas again and tried to imagine what it was like through Robyn's eyes. Lexi was proud of the piece, but it meant so much to her that Robyn saw exactly what she wanted to show. Beauty from darkness.

"I don't know. I just get these things in my head, and I need to get them out. I've missed it. The ideas, seeing my pieces come to life. I know it sounds dramatic, but my head is a very different place when I don't have that."

Robyn shook her head and turned toward Lexi.

"No, it's not dramatic. It's obvious. Watching you paint today, it's impossible not to see the effect it has on you. I may not fully understand, but it's undeniable. You glow."

Lexi wasn't quite sure when Robyn had gotten closer, but suddenly all she could think about was kissing her. She considered the fear that had kept her rooted earlier. And how Robyn spoke the words she needed to hear to push past that fear and make something amazing happen. And now Robyn was standing right in front of her, and Lexi didn't want fear to get in the way of anything else.

Lexi took their mostly empty plates and placed them on the coffee table. She turned back to Robyn and traced a finger along Robyn's hand and watched as Robyn's eyes briefly fluttered closed.

"I want to kiss you. I'm telling you, because so far being honest with you has worked in my favour today. I kind of think you want to kiss me too."

Robyn's mouth curled in a small smile as Lexi continued.

"If I'm wrong, we can binge-watch TV and pretend I said nothing. Well, that's probably unrealistic, I might be a little awkward for a minute, but I'll shake it off and it'll be business as usual. But if I'm right, maybe we can see what kissing would be like if it wasn't just to appease your family on a fake date?"

Lexi had barely finished the sentence before Robyn's lips were on hers. She wound her hands around Robyn's neck, parting her lips to allow Robyn's tongue the entry it desperately sought. She lay back against the couch and suddenly Robyn was all she could see, hear, taste, and feel. She threaded her hands into Robyn's hair and pulled her closer. As their kiss picked up the pace and the heat intensified, she felt Robyn's thigh move between her legs. Lexi's body responded enthusiastically, but her brain screeched to a halt. She moved her hands around to place them against Robyn's chest and pulled back.

Robyn shot up immediately. "Whoa, I'm sorry, Lex. I got way too carried away."

Lexi sat up, heart beating frantically as she took Robyn's hand in hers reassuringly.

"We both did. Probably because we are apparently very good at kissing."

Robyn laughed and Lexi leaned in to kiss her again, softly this time.

"I'm not ready for anything else right now. I know that's probably not what you're used to, and I understand if you want to cool the kissing altogether. But right now, that's all I can handle."

Robyn was stroking her finger across Lexi's hand, and it made Lexi's stomach clench. She didn't want to stop kissing Robyn, but she needed to be clear about where this was going tonight. Although her body was ready for whatever Robyn had to offer, Lexi knew her mind wasn't.

"So, what you're saying is I must endure endless kisses from a gorgeous woman? What a terrible position I've landed myself in."

Lexi swatted Robyn as she laughed.

"I'm being serious. If we kiss like we just did, it might be hard to stop. Things can be hard to keep in mind. But I don't want this to go any further right now, and I need to know you're okay with that."

Robyn held Lexi's gaze with a serious face.

"I would never want anything that you weren't comfortable with, Lexi. It's only good when it's good for us both. I have no doubt it would be good, but I mean that for during *and* after. Regrets aren't my thing. So, we could turn on the TV and just sit here together, or apart. Or if you want some good, old-fashioned teenage make-outs, I'm okay with that too. Just to be clear, my preference is option two."

In the end, they spent the better part of the evening kissing over and over, with the TV they pretended to watch in the background. Lexi couldn't think of a better way to spend her time.

CHAPTER ELEVEN

The rain was loud against the window as Robyn pulled her head up from her book. The scene was almost exactly the same as yesterday, yet it was infinitely different too. Robyn had awoken to the memory of Lexi's lips on hers still running through her mind. Her own lips tingled at the thought. Robyn had spent an extra few minutes in bed this morning reminiscing about the night before and relieving the pent-up tension in her body.

She had hoped it would take the edge off before she emerged from her room. But one glance at Lexi, the cause of the aching apex between her legs, had her throbbing once more. Lexi was already up and fixated on a new art piece as she joined her in the living room. Although Robyn meant everything she'd said last night, it had been a long time since she had spent hours kissing someone with nothing following. It was oddly thrilling, like savouring a meal before a long-awaited dessert.

Not knowing if dessert would ever be on the table, though—that was hard. Robyn was breaking all of her own rules by even considering going to bed with Lexi. Not only because they were roommates and friends, but because the longer they drew this out, the less it could be put down as a random action that they could go back to normal after. Whatever normal meant these days.

Robyn had gone about making them something to eat when she got up, knowing Lexi had likely dived right into her painting without bothering to make breakfast. It was good seeing Lexi back in front of the easel. The mess Robyn once tolerated with a hint of annoyance now filled her with happiness. It meant Lexi was creating, and having lived months without that happening, she would give up their whole apartment as a studio to make it continue.

Lexi had flashed her a grateful smile when she placed the food to her side and the fresh cup of tea, then went right back to what she was doing. That's what led to Robyn being back on the couch, enjoying the peaceful late morning reading her book and watching Lexi in between. It was new to her, how much she enjoyed witnessing Lexi paint. The simple actions of the brush, the images that formed seemingly from nowhere had become mesmerising. More than once she'd found herself rereading the same sentence because she had gotten distracted by Lexi. She could move so Lexi wouldn't be directly in her sight, but she didn't want to. Allowing herself to admit that was a big deal. Clearly, Lexi's straightforward honesty was rubbing off on her.

It was a couple of hours before Lexi turned and acknowledged Robyn again.

"Look!"

The excited exclamation made Robyn smile as she surveyed the piece Lexi had finished. It was good. Clean intricate lines formed what looked like people from one angle, and shapes from another. It didn't evoke the emotion in Robyn that the last piece had, but it was still impressive. Lexi was waiting expectantly.

"It looks great."

Lexi tilted her head, staring at Robyn. Robyn gulped, feeling like this was a test she hadn't studied for. She knew she wasn't reacting the way she had yesterday, but she also didn't want to pretend it affected her the same way. It was only day two of Lexi recapturing her creativity and the last thing Robyn wanted to do was hinder her progress with a lack of enthusiasm. But she thought pretence might cause the same outcome.

"I'm not going to break, Robbie. Be honest, please."

Lexi didn't seem worried, and Robyn had never had an issue being honest with her about these things before. Robyn wasn't an expert on anything art-related, but Lexi had asked for her opinion plenty of times and she'd given it, even when the opinion had been *I have no idea what that's supposed to be.*

"It really does look great. I like the colours, the three bits there stand out well. They kinda look like people when I look from this angle? And from the other side they look like weird shapes. So, I hope that's what you were going for."

Lexi nodded and moved her hand in a gesture for Robyn to continue.

"I know there's a but in there somewhere."

"No, not a but exactly. It just doesn't make me feel the same as that one did." Robyn gestured to the now dry canvas leaning against the wall at the side of the easel. Looking at it again brought the difference to light even more.

"I don't always get art, which you know. But that one... it made me feel things right away. Maybe it was because I saw how it started. The darkness that you somehow turned beautiful. But not by disguising it or hiding it or getting rid of it. You just used the light to accentuate it. Every time I look at it, I see new little pieces to admire. Those flowers down the side, that part up the top that looks a little like swirling flames. It's amazing. Maybe you just set the bar too high with it."

She shrugged her shoulders. Her cheeks were a little hot as she chanced a glance up at Lexi and continued. "That one looks like you poured your soul into it, and I hope you don't have plans for it because I really want it to stay in our apartment. This one is good and clean and looks like it would be hanging in a fancy hotel or something. That's all."

Robyn was relieved to see the smile on Lexi's face, not seeming disappointed with her observations at all. She stood rooted to her spot as Lexi walked toward her and wound her arms around Robyn's neck, raising up on her toes to plant a soft kiss on her mouth. As quickly as it had happened, it was over, as Lexi moved to place the canvas aside to dry.

"Wh-what was that for?"

Robyn was embarrassed at the break in her voice that betrayed her. She was used to being in control of herself, and in situations as a whole. The past couple of days with Lexi had made her feel totally out of control and she wasn't sure she minded.

"That's for being honest. I could see you struggling with how to say it and you managed it kindly. But you're exactly right. This one has approximately zero percent of my soul in it. It's the first of the corporate pieces I was commissioned for, and I may have sold out by taking the commissions, but my soul is staying far away from it."

Lexi placed another canvas on the easel and turned back toward Robyn.

"Oh, and that's exactly what they asked for. They wanted me to portray people to mean their employees, and also the geometric patterns that form their brand. I'm not in love with it, but it meets their requests, and it doesn't look awful. I was hoping the contrast of the angles would make it a little less boring."

Robyn nodded, brightening now that she understood.

"It's definitely not boring. It's not exactly emotive, but it's really clever. So, you did it?"

Robyn knew how concerned Lexi was with meeting this final deadline, not to mention that their rent depended on it too.

"Well, it's a start. They ordered several to showcase along their hallway, and I need to try to make each one unique enough. But a start is better than where I was."

Robyn picked her book back up and sat where she had been as Lexi mixed new colours. Lexi's blond hair was thrown up in a messy bun and she wore a string top that left the slope of her neck bare. Robyn followed the line with her eyes, imagining how it would feel to press her lips to each spot. She squirmed on the couch, the heat between her legs making things increasingly uncomfortable.

"When you're done watching me, do you want to answer your phone?"

Robyn's face flamed as she snapped out of her lust-induced daydream and heard the distant ringing of her phone, which was still on her bedside locker.

"I was reading my book," she huffed, as she got up and headed toward her room.

She rolled her eyes at the sass dripping from each word of Lexi's reply. "Sure, Robbie. You keep telling yourself that."

❖

Lexi couldn't remember the last time she had felt this good. Losing her creativity really made it hit home how much she took it for granted. She knew things weren't as straightforward as they had seemed before. It wasn't a switch that had been turned off and now it would stay on. A big part of her block had been the lack of interest in what she was creating, but that still didn't quite explain not being able to create anything at all because of it.

She hadn't forgotten what Sam had mentioned. In fact, she'd attempted to google more about ADHD and even about ADHD and creativity. There was so much information, too much, and it had quickly overwhelmed her. So, the searching stopped. Some of it had resonated, but other things not so much. How did people ever figure this stuff out? The parts about things being more interest-based for people with ADHD fit, and it got her thinking a lot about her art.

Lexi had been very lucky that up until recently, she had been able to follow her interests where they led her. Art had never been a struggle because it was never a chore, never a job. Until it had to be. Was she making the wrong decision, trying to turn her favourite thing into a career? Would it ruin the love of it for her? She couldn't imagine spending her days doing anything else. The thought of sitting in an office for hours and pretending to care about making other people money terrified her. So many people had no choice in that, and she was thankful she did. But the self-imposed pressure had added more bricks to the walls that had surrounded her creativity.

Now the walls were falling, and Lexi had woken with a head full of ideas that morning, and she hadn't wasted a minute. As she put the finishing touches on the third commissioned piece, she put down the paintbrush, finally feeling safe enough that she'd be able to pick it back up the next day and continue. She had a brief temptation to stay up through the night and finish as much as she could before the ideas dried out. However, Robyn's eyes, still focused on her, were more tempting.

Lexi was full of pent-up energy, relief from her achievements, and memories of the night before. As she finished tidying her supplies and glanced at Robyn, the buzzing under her skin intensified. Robyn was in her sports tank top and tight black leggings, using the pull-up bar she had attached to her bedroom doorway. With Robyn's career, working out was a daily occurrence. One that Lexi had witnessed on numerous occasions. But seeing the muscles along Robyn's arms and shoulder blades flex as she pulled herself up, in a move Lexi would never manage, now had her mouth watering.

She had always admired Robyn's strength, but right now it had her imagining other things Robyn could do with those muscles. It was a little astounding how the same action, that weeks ago would have pulled nothing more than admiration from her, now ignited her body. Lexi leaned back against the edge of the couch and watched, not wanting to pull her eyes away from the sight. As if sensing an audience, Robyn flipped her hands on the bar and turned to face her, in a swift motion Lexi guessed was far harder than Robyn made it look. A confident grin danced on Robyn's face as she did two more pull-ups.

Her shirt rode up and Lexi allowed her gaze to wander to the toned muscles on display under the thin fabric. Before today, she had no idea she could be attracted to someone's abdomen. Robyn let go of the bar and they both stood, staring at one another. Robyn's breathing was quick from the exertion, and Lexi's followed pace. It was like a game of chicken, a challenge of who would blink first. Lexi was learning about a lot of new things that could be attractive, including staring into the eyes of someone who made no attempt to hide the fact that they were undressing you in their head.

Neither spoke, but they both moved simultaneously. Suddenly, Lexi was against a wall and Robyn's mouth was on hers in a move that sent shockwaves through the most sensitive parts of her body. Her brain filled with relief, the kind you get from that first sip of ice-cold water in the blistering heat. They were kissing and it was like everything she remembered from the night before but so much more.

Lexi's arms wrapped around Robyn's neck, and before she even knew what had happened, Robyn gripped her ass and she instinctively wrapped her legs around Robyn's waist. She had a momentary thought of how she was sure that only happened in romance movies, before the friction of being pressed against Robyn's waist had her throwing her head back and biting back a moan. The thin fabric of her loose cotton shorts was doing nothing to hide the heat radiating between her legs.

Robyn's lips were on her neck and Lexi gripped her hair, holding her in place as she rocked against her, the ache intensifying with every movement. Robyn's fingers dug into the skin of her ass holding her tight, and Lexi was sure she would combust on the spot. They were both still fully clothed, Robyn had yet to touch her, and even so, Lexi was closer than she had ever been to climaxing without help from her own fingers.

Robyn pulled back and Lexi opened her eyes, already missing the feel of her lips. They both stared at each other again, with heavy breathing and swollen lips.

"Fuck, Lexi."

Robyn's voice was little more than a strained whisper, but the words rippled through Lexi as she followed it up with a head shake.

"What are you doing to me?"

"I'm the one with my back against the wall and my legs wrapped around your waist, so I think that's a question I should be asking."

Lexi unhooked her legs as Robyn let go of the grip she had on her ass. Robyn moved her hands to Lexi's waist instead, to keep them pressed together. Lexi was grateful for that because she wasn't so sure she was ready to stand completely of her own volition yet. Robyn ducked her head to graze Lexi's lips softly and pulled back as Lexi groaned.

Robyn chuckled. "Why are you pouting?"

"Because you're no longer kissing me."

Lexi exaggerated the pout and Robyn leaned in again to bite her bottom lip softly, sucking it into her mouth. How Lexi had gone so long without experiencing this was something she would never understand.

"Well, somebody has a just-kissing rule. And if we continued the way we were going, that rule would have been broken. So, I'm being safe."

Lexi was barely following Robyn's words. The lust-filled haze that engulfed her was not conducive to comprehension.

"That was yesterday's rule. Plus, aren't rules meant to be broken?"

Lexi batted her eyelashes and widened her eyes as Robyn groaned.

"Sunny, you're not playing fair. I'm trying to respect your wishes. The wishes you made clear when you still had some of your wits about you."

Lexi switched their positions in a smooth action she thanked her years of dance lessons for. Robyn's mouth opened in a small circle as her back pressed against the wall with Lexi in front of her, hands pressed to her hips.

"My name is Alexis Kathleen Lynch. I'm twenty-eight years old. I have a degree in Fine Art and currently have all my wits about me. You, Robyn Anne Moore, respected my wishes last night. So, if it's okay with you, I'd like you to respect them again."

Robyn visibly gulped and Lexi loved how much she affected her.

"And what are your wishes? What do you want?"

Robyn was asking if she was sure, giving her time to change her mind. It made Lexi want her even more.

"My wishes right now are for you to take me to your room and finish what we started. I want you, Robyn."

CHAPTER TWELVE

Robyn needed no further instructions. The minute she heard Lexi's words, she took her hand and pulled her a few feet to her bedroom. She was glad she had tidied up before grabbing her gym equipment earlier. The room was bright with light streaming through the window. She had momentarily forgotten it was still daytime. She walked to the window and pulled the curtains closed.

Their apartment was on the third floor, so it was unlikely they would have any witnesses. But now that she had Lexi willing and ready in her room, Robyn was nervous and stalling. She hadn't been in this position, not since she was a teenager at least. Lexi came up behind her and wrapped her arms around Robyn's waist as she kissed her way along Robyn's shoulder, dissipating her nerves with every kiss.

Robyn turned in Lexi's arms, moving her thumbs along the curve of Lexi's hip bone. She gripped the edge of Lexi's string top, the thin fabric doing little to conceal the evidence of Lexi's arousal. She pulled it up and off in one swift motion. Lexi wasn't wearing a bra, something Robyn had been aware of but not fully prepared for. Her exposed breasts were soft beneath Robyn's touch as she glided her fingers along the skin, in contrast to the hardened nipples that ached for attention. Something Robyn was more than happy to provide.

Robyn dipped her head, pulling one between her lips and sucking gently as she kneaded the other breast. The sounds emanating from Lexi had Robyn picking up pace, desperate to hear more. She moved her thumb and forefinger to pinch Lexi's nipple softly, applying pressure little by little to gauge her reaction. As Robyn grazed her teeth along the nipple in her mouth, Lexi's fingers dug into her shoulders and she whimpered louder this time.

Robyn lifted her head and whispered softly, "You okay?"

Sex wasn't a one-kind-fits-all type of situation, and Robyn wanted to make sure that her intuition was leading her down the right track. Lexi nodded and pushed Robyn's head back to where it had been, giving her all the reassurance she needed. Robyn moved to the other side, swirling her tongue around the now swollen nipple and pulling it between her teeth. She applied more pressure this time as she moved her hand down Lexi's stomach, caressing every inch of skin it passed along the way.

Lexi's knees buckled briefly as Robyn's fingers grazed beneath the waistband of her shorts. Robyn halted her movements and stood, walking Lexi back until they reached the bed. Lexi tugged at Robyn's tank top until Robyn pulled both that and her sports bra over her head. She dropped them to the floor and bit her lip, almost groaning at the image before her. Lexi was kneeling on the bed in front of Robyn, staring at her with widened eyes.

Robyn was thankful she had only begun her workout when Lexi distracted her, or she would be far more concerned with forgoing a shower first. And now, the idea of Lexi joining her in the shower was top of her wish list. But Lexi grabbed Robyn's hips and pulled her close, and thoughts of the shower faded. Lexi dipped her head and paid as much attention to Robyn's breasts as Robyn had to hers. Robyn's nipples had never been particularly sensitive, but the way Lexi worshipped them had her aching more than ever before. Her clit was throbbing, and she was sure her underwear was soaked through at this point. Lexi hadn't even grazed below her belly button yet, but Robyn could feel her everywhere. Lexi moved her tongue down Robyn's abdomen and along the top of her very damp leggings. Lexi's hand pressed on top of the fabric between the warmth of Robyn's thighs, and she tilted her head to look up at Robyn.

Robyn was captivated by the image. *So damn beautiful.* Lexi's hair framed her face, and her pink cheeks were flushed with arousal. Her eyes were lighter than usual and Lexi placed more pressure against her swollen clit. Robyn kissed her deeply, a moan escaping her mouth.

"Lex, if you keep that up, this is going to end far too soon."

Lexi grinned, ignoring Robyn's pleas as she picked up the pace of her movements. Robyn rocked against her automatically, seeking the friction her body needed. She dug her fingers into Lexi's shoulders, sure her nails would leave marks but unable to let go if she tried. All the while, Lexi kept her eyes trained on Robyn's face.

Robyn's legs began to shake, and she stopped resisting the tidal wave that was ready to wash over her. The orgasm ripped through her thighs and core, curling in her stomach as she let out strangled cries. Lexi held her up with one hand curled around her back and the other hand between Robyn's legs, her movements slowing as Robyn came down. She opened her eyes, and the look on Lexi's face was almost enough to have her climbing back up again. Her smug smile radiated pride.

"Lexi. Fuck."

Lexi pulled Robyn down to kiss her softly before whispering, "You forgot something very important."

Robyn mumbled an unintelligible response, as Lexi

moved her mouth to Robyn's navel, circling her tongue around slowly before dipping it inside.

"You coming for me isn't the end of anything. That was just the beginning."

Robyn melted, and before she knew it, she and Lexi had traded places. As Robyn sat on the bed, Lexi slowly removed her leggings and knelt on the floor in front of her. It was all far too surreal. Robyn wasn't used to this. She wasn't used to being the first one to come undone, she was used to causing the undoing. Now Lexi's mouth was working its way up Robyn's thigh, and she had yet to regain her breathing from the first time. It caught her completely off guard, but in the best possible way.

Lexi glanced up and their eyes locked for a moment.

"I've never done this before." The husky tone of Lexi's voice sent shockwaves of pleasure through Robyn. She tried to gain control of herself to reply.

"You don't have to. We can slow it down."

Lexi shook her head emphatically.

"God, no. I want to. Just…let me know if you need me to change anything. Okay?"

Robyn bit her lip to stop a groan, the aching between her legs intensifying with the eagerness on Lexi's face.

"I will but I won't need to. You've managed very damn well already."

Lexi looked at her with longing written all over her face and Robyn couldn't tear her eyes away. Lexi reached her tongue out and flicked it across Robyn's most sensitive spot, still retaining eye contact. It was, by far, one of the hottest experiences of Robyn's life. Suddenly, Lexi closed her eyes and started to devour her in a way that had Robyn clenching the sheets tight beneath her hands and biting her lip to keep from screaming louder than the neighbours would appreciate.

Lexi wrapped her arms around both of Robyn's thighs, pulling her closer as she pushed her tongue deep inside, bringing Robyn to the edge over and over before switching positions. Right when Robyn thought she couldn't take any more, Lexi moved her lips back to her aching clit and pulled it into her mouth. Lexi sucked hard as she pushed two fingers deep inside Robyn and curled them. Robyn's thighs clenched around Lexi's head, and no amount of lip biting could stop the sounds that came from deep inside her body as she tumbled over the blissful edge.

❖

Lexi had been sure as Robyn orgasmed above her that it was the best view in the world. But lying with her head against Robyn's bare thigh, looking up over the curve of her naked breasts and watching her eyes drift shut, she wasn't sure she could choose. The satiated look on Robyn's face was one she wouldn't get out of her head for a long time, and she loved being the cause of it.

Lexi had worried momentarily about the fact that Robyn was far more experienced than she was. That she wouldn't know what to do. But the minute she had seen Robyn's naked body in front of her, everything else fell away. The idea of exploring her body in every way possible was all Lexi could think about.

Lexi's arm was slung across Robyn's stomach, and Robyn was running her fingers in a gentle back and forth rhythm across it. She allowed her own eyes to shut briefly as she revelled in the peaceful moment. The ache between her legs was still present, but she wasn't rushing this. She was content to relax and enjoy the quiet hum of her body.

That was, until her stomach rumbled embarrassingly loud.

Her eyes flew wide, and Robyn was looking at her, an amused look on her face.

"I think your body is requesting nourishment."

"My body is requesting a lot of things." Lexi waggled her eyebrows as she replied, and Robyn's eyes darkened.

"And I want to oblige all of your body's requests. But I just realised you haven't eaten since the food I gave you this morning, so we're dealing with that first."

Robyn made to move off the bed and Lexi pouted, ready to argue. But at her stomach's next loud protestation she relented and followed Robyn to the kitchen. Robyn had grabbed a T-shirt on their way out that barely covered her ass, which made focusing on food a lot more difficult. She swatted Lexi's hand away and pointed a finger at her, using the stern voice Lexi imagined she generally reserved for her trainees.

"Food first."

Lexi brought her hand up in salute and replied, "Yes, Captain!"

Robyn rolled her eyes and bit back a laugh. "Captain, really?"

Lexi shrugged, piling leftovers from the previous night's take-out into a dish and popping it in the oven to heat. The microwave would be quicker, but the oven tasted better, and Lexi didn't like to compromise on the quality of day-old fast food.

"I don't know all the lingo. You told me you'd be getting some promotion. Does that mean I get to call you Captain?"

Robyn didn't hide her laugh this time. "I said I applied for the promotion. I haven't gotten it yet. And no, my title won't be Captain. You watch too much American TV."

"You didn't say I couldn't call you Captain, though."

Lexi used her best flirty tone and ran her finger along the hem of Robyn's T-shirt. It had the exact effect she was hoping for. Robyn pulled her into a deep kiss, then picked her up and placed her on the countertop.

"You're far too good at lifting me," Lexi said in a breathy tone.

Her legs were open, and Robyn was standing between them with her lips on Lexi's neck as she mumbled a reply. "I knew the workouts would come in handy someday."

Robyn kissed her way up to Lexi's earlobe, sucking softly before whispering, "How long does that food need to heat?"

Robyn's hands were already pulling at Lexi's shorts, and she helped the process along by removing them.

"Why, not hungry?" Lexi's teasing tone ended on a whimper as Robyn captured her lips before pulling her hips to the edge of the countertop and dropping to her knees in front of Lexi.

"Starving."

It was lucky Lexi had put the food down low because it ended up heating far longer than it needed to. Eventually, she lay against Robyn on the couch with all her body's requests fulfilled. Her mind had been uncharacteristically peaceful up until then, but it started to fill with thoughts again. Thoughts that bubbled out before her brain could fully form them.

"That's never happened before, by the way."

Robyn had been stroking her back softly and the movement paused, then continued.

"Someone going down on you on a countertop?"

Lexi poked Robyn's side but kept her head against her chest. Talking was easier like this. She was naked and lying on top of Robyn, but speaking about these things somehow made her feel more vulnerable.

"No. Well, yes. But that's not what I meant. I just...I've never orgasmed like that before. Usually it's me, myself, and I when that happens."

Robyn kissed the top of her head, and Lexi appreciated the comfort of the gesture.

"How did it feel?"

It wasn't the response she was expecting. It was a simple question. Not one of shock, or bravado, or disbelief. Robyn asked as if it was all that mattered to her.

"Amazing. Honestly, I wasn't sure it was something I would ever experience."

Robyn's hand moved from her back to her neck, massaging softly as she spoke. "Why not?"

"I'm demisexual. I don't really feel any type of strong attraction unless I already care about someone. This type of passion has never happened for me before. I was beginning to think it was all a fairy tale. An X-rated, not for kids, kinda fairy tale."

Robyn chuckled and Lexi smiled at the sound.

"If it hadn't happened, would you have been disappointed?"

Robyn shifted to pull Lexi up and cupped her face. "Sunny, why would I be disappointed?" Robyn's eyes searched hers, concern etched on her face.

"Well, because that's the end goal, right? I was worried I'd bruise that big ego of yours if I couldn't…"

It was true that Lexi had worried about that when they got started. But by the time she was on the counter, Lexi hadn't been focused on anything but how good Robyn made her feel. Robyn kissed her then. A soft, slow kiss that was so much more with the vulnerability of the moment.

"I care about making you feel good. I care about pleasuring you. But making you come isn't the only way, or the most important thing to me. Did I love watching you let go for me? Very, very much. Would I have been disappointed if I got to spend the whole time between your legs, hearing you call my name and moan in pleasure until we were both too exhausted to move? No way in hell."

Lexi barely let Robyn finish speaking before she kissed her again. Robyn's words meant so much more than she understood. Lexi had been single for so long, mostly due to devoting her time to art. But also because she had never felt drawn to anyone the way she felt drawn to Robyn. It had always seemed like too much effort and like it would take her away from her painting. But with Robyn, it didn't feel like trying.

As their thighs slid together and their bodies moved as one, Lexi was filled with more passion than she had ever experienced in her life. She had no idea what this meant, what they were. She could barely believe that it was only yesterday that she had confronted what she wanted and allowed herself to flirt with Robyn.

How naive she had been, thinking they could see where things went and revert back to normalcy after. Not even thirty-six hours later, and she knew for sure, nothing would ever be normal again. Lexi had always felt her feelings big, right there on her sleeve for the world to see. But these feelings were covering her whole body, and they were bigger than she had room to process right now.

After they had both exploded again in a sea of ecstasy at almost the same time, she lay in Robyn's arms and listened to her soft snores. Her brain was racing with all the possibilities, all the things they hadn't discussed before diving off this cliff. She was certain of one thing: If she had the chance to rewind a few hours and do it all again, she'd leap off headfirst without a second thought. She nestled closer, and Robyn's grip tightened around her even as she slept.

CHAPTER THIRTEEN

The engine rolled into the station after a particularly nasty call to the scene of a car accident. The whole crew were quiet, despondent. Everyone was mostly uninjured apart from the passenger, a barely-school-age little kid, who hadn't been in great shape when they got them to the hospital. Robyn would have a hard time getting the mother's screams out of her head, or the image of the tiny body she was sure couldn't have survived, before they found a weak pulse.

After grabbing a shower with still another few hours left in her shift, Robyn hit the treadmill in their gym room. Tommy joined her not long after and they ran side by side in silence for a while.

"I saw you with that hot new nurse when we were leaving the hospital. Back in the saddle already?"

He waggled his eyebrows as Robyn rolled her eyes. Leave it to Tommy to push past the sadness of the day and go straight to gossip.

She had finally gotten an answer to the niggling in the back of her head as she left the hospital and bumped into Ollie, Dani's friend from the bar.

"Stop objectifying women, you sound like a creep. She has a name."

Tommy held both hands up while keeping steady pace.

"Sorry. The new nurse who you're apparently on a first-name basis with already. You move fast, dude."

"She's a friend of a friend. I bumped into her the other night at Blaze, and it was bothering me trying to figure out how I knew her face. She's been working at the hospital for the past few months, so I've likely run into her a few times. I'm terrible at recognizing people outside of their uniforms, though."

The minute the words left her mouth she regretted them as Tommy sputtered a laugh.

"That's funny, since you've definitely gotten a fair few of them out of those uniforms throughout the years."

Robyn upped the speed on the treadmill, hoping the sound of the blood pumping in her ears would drown him out. "Either pick a different topic or learn to keep some of your thoughts in your head."

There was silence for a moment and Robyn relished the peace.

"So, you jump your fake girlfriend's bones yet?"

"Really, Brenn? That's what you call changing topic?"

She couldn't be mad, though, not really. She knew it was his way of getting them past this. Calls involving kids were always harder. If they dwelled on things for too long, they'd never go back out there. Joking, gossiping, making their downtime as light-hearted as possible, that's what got them through the darker parts of their job.

"You totally did." He exaggerated the words in mock horror.

Robyn kept her mouth shut and stopped the machine. She grabbed a towel to clean it down and Tommy did the same. He clearly intended not to let her off the hook.

"One fake date does not a fake girlfriend make," she shot

over her shoulder as they walked toward the canteen to grab food.

"Oh, so you've told your mom you're not dating?"

Robyn sighed. She hated when he had a point. They crashed on the couch with snacks, and she took a moment, tossing up between a change of subject versus getting advice.

"Okay, no. And she asked to meet for dinner on Friday. *Both* of us. I haven't spoken to Lexi about it yet, but I'm not sure now is the time for that."

"Because you got it on?"

Robyn took a moment, then closed her eyes and nodded.

"I knew it! So, what's the problem? It's not fake anymore. You can go be all gooey eyed—your mom will eat that shit up."

If only things were that simple. After spending a couple of days with Lexi in blissful domesticity, Robyn was beginning to think maybe they could be more than roommates. She had awoken this morning and they were still wrapped up together on the couch. The sun was beginning to stream through a small gap in the living room curtains. Lexi was curled against her side, which made it far harder for Robyn to move. She had never been late or missed a shift in her career, but it was the first time she was tempted to, if only to not disturb Lexi's peaceful slumber.

As Robyn had inched out from beneath her, Lexi expelled the cutest grumble and settled back against the cushion. It had been late by the time they'd finally fallen to sleep, after she had awoken to Lexi's lips on her neck again. They hadn't really discussed staying on the couch. They both had perfectly good beds they could have relocated to. But for some reason, suggesting going to bed together just to sleep was a much bigger thing than falling asleep together on the couch. And it was clear neither of them had wanted to go to bed alone.

It had been a long shift, but the late night had been worth every exhausted moment. The text from her mother had been on her phone as she grabbed her stuff to leave this morning. As she had taken one last look toward a still sleeping Lexi, she considered the scenario. How would the conversation even go? She couldn't ask Lexi to come to dinner as her fake girlfriend, not after the night they'd just shared. But it was far too soon to ask her to dinner with her mom as her real girlfriend.

Real girlfriend.

Robyn's heart thrummed at the words as they stuck in her head. Robyn had been out and proud as a lesbian since she was a teenager, and yet she had never had one of those. Not for lack of chance—there had been girls and then women throughout the years that had wanted things to go that way. But Robyn had never before considered the possibility. Not after seeing what love did to her mother, what loss could create. Nobody had been worth that risk. So why did the thought suddenly make her stomach flip?

"Earth to Red. Where'd you go?"

Robyn snapped back to attention, focusing on the hand waving in front of her face.

"Sorry, I was just thinking about it all. Mainly how I navigate the newness of the actual relationship with the lie my mother believes."

Tommy's eyes went wide, and he pressed the back of his hand to Robyn's forehead. Robyn swatted him away.

"Sorry, just checking for a fever. You said the word *relationship*, so one of us is clearly delirious."

"You're such an ass."

Tommy shrugged and then put on his big brother face, which meant the conversation was about to get more serious.

"Seriously, though, is that what this is? A relationship? You know I've been bugging you to settle down, if only because your game makes me jealous, but it seems a little sudden. You already live together...how does that work?"

Tommy was asking the question that had been running through Robyn's head since she left the comfort of their carefree bubble and entered back into the real world. They should've discussed these things before anything happened, but there hadn't been a chance in hell she was stopping for a conversation when Lexi had made clear what she wanted at that moment. The text from her mom had brought reality back, and the devastation at the car crash had triggered the worry and fear that left room for doubt to creep back in again. Surprisingly, it didn't have Robyn running for the hills immediately, and that was something to be noted.

They talked a little more, though Robyn didn't have any answers to give. She made it clear Tommy wasn't saying anything she hadn't been thinking to herself, and they played a few games of pool before leaving. They'd be back on shift together in another fifteen hours, so she promised she'd do her best to talk to Lexi before then. As Robyn drove the short journey home, she passed Blaze, the bar name lighting up like a beacon.

After a shift like she'd just had, it's where she would usually end up. She'd have left her car at the station, pushed past the tiredness she could already feel overcoming her, and gone to grab a drink. Then she would have ended up in someone's bed, only to roll out of there before the sun came up and head back to the station for her next shift. The thought didn't bring the same tug that it usually did, the impulse to lose herself in a stranger and switch off her feelings. Instead, something was tugging her home, to her apartment, where feelings didn't come with an off switch.

And Robyn knew exactly what was doing the tugging... her heart.

❖

It had been a fruitful day for Lexi. As she stood and reviewed the canvases placed against the wall, she smiled, relief overcoming her. It was the week of her final deadline, and she had all but one piece complete. She had taken photos of the current pieces and forwarded them to the company liaison who had placed the order. The email that landed in her inbox was very positive—they were a hit. Even if they weren't Lexi's favourite pieces, the client was happy, and that's what mattered.

She had considered going to the studio that day. She'd have the space to set up multiple pieces and work between them, which often worked well if she was stuck. But something inside her was still afraid to mess up her current flow. This lone easel in the corner of her small living room had worked so far, so why tempt fate? Although the studio was a better set-up in theory, Lexi was realizing that being in the place where her passion had flared the most spurred her on.

Lexi still found herself glancing over to the spot on the couch where Robyn had spent much of the previous two days. Although the couch was now vacant, the memory of catching Robyn watching her still made her happy. She imagined Robyn's eyes on her as she moved the brush along the canvas. Art had always been a very solitary activity for Lexi, but even the memory of Robyn watching her had her hand moving with renewed vigour. Her newfound passion for Robyn combined with her revived passion for painting filled her with an excitement beyond anything she had felt before.

As she washed up in the bathroom, the door opened and shut. Her heart squeezed in anticipation of seeing Robyn.

Thoughts raced through her mind about how things would be. It had been easy the past couple of days to get lost in the haze of lust and excitement, but would it be different now that they'd spent the day apart? Part of Lexi had wondered if Robyn would return at all after shift. It wasn't always a given, and they hadn't made any agreements to the contrary. She decided to hold on to the excitement that had been coursing through her moments ago and let it guide her.

When Lexi walked into the living room, Robyn was sitting on the couch, eyes closed. Her shoulders were slumped, as if the weight of the world pulled her under. Lexi stood for a moment, unsure if her presence would be a welcome disturbance, before chastising herself. This was still Robyn, her friend, if nothing more. She walked over and sat beside her, taking Robyn's hand in hers. Robyn's eyes fluttered open, and a small smile appeared on her lips.

"Hey."

The way the soft word was uttered proved her suspicion. Robyn was bone tired. She ran a hand across Robyn's cheek, and Robyn nestled into the touch. It wasn't often she saw Robyn like this. Usually, if Robyn came home after a difficult shift, she would retreat to her room and spend time alone before eventually sleeping. Occasionally, Lexi would knock and offer food, but most of the time she would leave Robyn be. That wasn't happening this time, though, not unless Robyn specifically requested it.

"Hey yourself. You okay?"

Robyn's nod said yes, but her face said no. Creases formed on her forehead and her eyelids were heavy.

"Car crash. There was a kid involved, it was bad. I did good at pushing it aside until now, but my brain is too tired to block out the images."

Lexi hated the sadness that clung to Robyn. Grief for a stranger she would likely never see again but cared about all the same.

"What do you need?"

Robyn gave a half shrug before replying, "I showered and ate at the station, so I'm good on those fronts. We should probably talk, though, right?"

They should. Lexi knew that too. But it would be futile with Robyn in no state for rational conversation.

"We will. But not tonight. You need sleep."

Robyn tightened her grip on Lexi's hand. "I will. I just need to switch off first."

It had never occurred to Lexi before that the reason Robyn didn't go right to sleep after such a tiring shift was because of the images that replayed when she closed her eyes. That's why she binge-watched mindless shows or lost herself to fantasy worlds in the books she went through faster than anyone Lexi knew. Robyn needed to switch the memories off so she could sleep.

"Can I help?"

Robyn didn't let people take care of her. It was a fact Lexi had been aware of since very early on. Where Lexi wore her heart on her sleeve, Robyn was a closed book. The very few times she had ever seen Robyn sick, she would hardly leave her bedroom. But Lexi was taking advantage of this unknown state they found themselves in, hoping Robyn would accept her offer.

The vulnerability in Robyn's eyes as she stared at Lexi before responding was raw, rare, and so very beautiful. She weighed things up in her head before eventually nodding and mumbling a quiet *please*. Lexi stood, tugging Robyn with her, and walked toward Robyn's bedroom. She had a feeling Robyn would be more comfortable in her own space, plus her room was the bigger of the two and she had a TV on the wall across from her bed, something Lexi hadn't bothered with since she spent more of her time in the living room.

She grabbed Robyn's pyjamas and handed them to her, instructing her to change while she went to get her own. Although her body wanted to help Robyn switch off in a very different way, right now she wanted to take this opportunity to comfort Robyn, no strings attached. She flicked the kettle on before getting changed, then made them both tea and grabbed Robyn's favourite chocolate biscuits for comfort food. Robyn was lying under the covers when she returned, lost in her thoughts. Her face lit up when Lexi handed her the warm mug and shook the packet of biscuits.

Lexi set her own mug on the bedside table and grabbed the remote, turning on the TV. Pushing past any niggling concerns, she pulled back the covers and slid in beside Robyn. The grateful look that spread across Robyn's face eased all of Lexi's doubts as she flicked through the streaming channels.

"So, what'll it be, sapphic serial killer, sapphic vampire, or sapphic sheriff?"

Robyn grinned and sipped her tea.

"You pick."

Lexi pressed play on an episode they'd already seen, knowing Robyn wouldn't have energy to concentrate on new information. After they'd finished their tea and polished off half the packet of biscuits, Robyn's eyelids began to flutter closed. They flew back open a couple minutes later, and that troubled expression returned to her face.

Lexi extended an arm and Robyn moved under it. She stroked Robyn's hair gently in a slow, soothing rhythm until she heard the soft snores indicating Robyn had finally succumbed to sleep. Lexi waited a little while longer, keeping the movements going until she was sure Robyn was out for the count. She slid down and turned, wrapped her other arm around Robyn, and cuddled close.

The intimacy of the night was completely different to the previous, yet somehow ended up making her feel even closer to Robyn. She wondered momentarily if this was the point where she should get up and go to her own bed, content that Robyn was at ease. But no part of her was willing to move from the comfort of Robyn's embrace.

CHAPTER FOURTEEN

It was the second morning in a row that Robyn woke up tangled up in Lexi, except this time it was in her own bed. As her eyes blinked open, Lexi was staring back at her, a faraway look on her face.

"Morning, Sunny." Her throat was dry, and her voice cracked.

Lexi broke out of her daydream and smiled. "Morning. How're you feeling?"

Robyn flashed back to the night before. When she had walked into the apartment and heard Lexi in the bathroom, she'd sat on the couch for a moment. Her intention had been to wait for Lexi and ask to talk about things. The exhaustion that had descended upon her the minute she sat down was unexpected. She had been running on adrenaline until she reached the comfort of her home. Her plans to talk had been trashed, but Lexi had taken care of her. More than that, Robyn had *allowed* Lexi to take care of her.

It was a foreign feeling, a distant memory, being taken care of. One she hadn't let herself indulge in for a long time. The feelings that came bubbling to the surface because of it were tangled and messy and she would have to find some time to figure those out. But right now, she had a shift to get to.

"I'm okay. I gotta grab a shower and run to work, though."

Lexi nodded, then her eyes dropped to Robyn's mouth and back up, hesitant. Robyn took the initiative and leaned in, grazing her lips against Lexi's softly. What she had meant to be a quick peck evolved into a heated kiss. Lexi pulled her closer and Robyn moved on top, aching to feel Lexi's skin against hers.

"Do you really have to shower?" Lexi mumbled between kisses.

Robyn flashed back to the imaginary wish list she'd started after Lexi's bathroom teasing.

"I do," she began, pulling back from Lexi to stand. She saw the disappointment that flashed across Lexi's face. "But you could join me."

Lexi's features changed as she nodded her agreement and followed Robyn to the bathroom. They shed their pyjamas along the way. Robyn got the shower started and stepped inside. She pulled Lexi beneath the cascading water and pressed their bodies together, kissing her until neither of them could breathe. Shock and desire flashed through Robyn as Lexi nudged her to face the shower wall.

She placed her palms flat against the surface as Lexi spread her legs from behind, running a hand between them. She gasped as Lexi pinched her clit, then plunged two fingers inside her and wrapped her other hand around to knead her breasts. She bit her lip, moving back to meet each thrust as the tightness curled in her stomach. She dropped her head and let out a string of unintelligible words as Lexi added a third finger, picking up her pace.

When Lexi's teeth sank into the soft skin of her shoulder, Robyn saw stars. Pleasure rippled through every part of her body and she fell against the wall. Lexi's arms wrapped around Robyn and pulled her back, holding her tight. Robyn turned in her arms and they kissed again, slowly this time. She was running low on time, but there wasn't a chance she was leaving before seeing Lexi come undone for her again.

The idea of showering together to save time was clearly not well thought out. As Robyn threw clothes on after returning the favour, twice, Lexi handed her a to-go cup. Robyn flashed on how strange and yet how normal it all was. Waking up together, morning sex, then Lexi making her tea as she left for work. It was oddly domestic. Before she ran out the door, a thought occurred to her. She blurted it out before she had time to reconsider.

"My mom invited us both to dinner on Friday. I have to run, but maybe we can talk about it later?"

Lexi looked a little startled, but she smiled and nodded as Robyn headed out. She knew she had sort of ambushed Lexi with the information, but it hadn't been an outright no, so that was a good sign, right? She shot her mom a reply to say she'd check with Lexi and get back to her. It would keep her at bay for the moment, otherwise her phone was bound to start ringing.

"Look who decided to show her face."

She was only ten minutes late for shift. It wasn't a big deal, except it had never happened before, so it was noticeable. She caught a few of her colleagues glancing at her as she threw her stuff in her locker.

"I'm barely late."

"Uh-huh. I wonder what could have possibly kept you. I'm guessing the talk went well, then?"

Robyn's cheeks flamed and she grabbed a controller for the gaming console they had set up in the rec room. She tossed a second one to Tommy and started up a round of *Mario Kart*.

"Hush and pick your character. I have a reputation to uphold."

"Which reputation are we talking about?" Tommy said as

the race began. Robyn shot past him, straight to first place, leaving a banana in her wake that Tommy predictably stumbled over.

"My reputation at kicking your ass in this game every damn time. Why do you even keep playing? It's getting a little sad."

They spent the next hour playing until the alarms blared and they jumped into action. On the days where very little happened, she often wished for more to keep the boredom at bay. But after yesterday, she was hoping for low drama today. Someone locked out of their house, even a cat in a tree would keep her happy. Okay, that wasn't a thing, but still. They geared up and jumped in the truck. As the address got called out again, she froze. *Wait, what?*

"Isn't that your building?"

Tommy confirmed that she hadn't misheard, and Robyn's insides turned to ice. *No.* It was ridiculous to jump right to worst case scenarios. They lived in a building with many other tenants. There were multiple reasons they got called out to apartments, surprisingly few of which were fires. Most likely this had absolutely nothing to do with Lexi. No matter how many times she told herself this, her heart didn't seem to get the memo. The beating got faster as they zipped through traffic, the journey taking far longer than it should with their sirens blaring.

She only realised her hands were shaking when Tommy placed his own on top of them, halting their movements. He squeezed and gave her a reassuring nod that she couldn't return. They rounded the last corner, and she glanced out the window, trying to see if there was any smoke to be seen. Smoke didn't always indicate fire, but the opposite was generally true. Nothing obvious jumped out at her and her heart slowed a bit, not yet returning to its normal pace. A lot of her neighbours were milling around outside, but Robyn hadn't glimpsed Lexi yet. The racing likely wouldn't stop until she laid eyes on her.

She jumped out of the truck as it pulled in front of her building. Every instinct she had was screaming at her to run into the building, but she stopped and awaited instruction. When she heard that the alarm was sounding from her apartment, her head swivelled in all directions. Still not seeing Lexi, she couldn't contain herself any longer.

"Officer Milton, that's my place. My…my roommate might be in there."

She was hoping it would speed up the process. They had procedures for a reason, and she had never wanted to break them before this moment. There was a reason they didn't go diving headfirst into potential fires before the commanding officer assessed the scene, and it was for the safety of them and others. But the smoke alarm going off meant smoke. Smoke likely meant fire. And Lexi could be trapped.

"Okay, Moore, you're sitting this one out. Everyone else, grab your gear and head up. Is there anything we should be aware of, likely obstacles or blockages?"

Robyn wanted to scream. She had never in her life disobeyed a direct command, or even argued one.

"No, it should be clear. Please, sir, I know my way around. If there's a fire, I'm your best asset."

She began grabbing her stuff as her colleagues raced in. Officer Milton stood in front of her, blocking her path.

"Tools down, Moore. Go hook up the hose in case we need it and stay out of that building, understand?"

Anger raged inside her, but she did as she was told, her heart in her throat the whole time. As she stood watching the door for any movement, she heard her name and turned, relief flooding through her. Lexi was running toward her from the top of the street, a confused look on her face and a grocery bag in hand. As she got closer, Robyn grabbed her, pulling her tight.

"What's going on? What happened?"

Robyn stepped back, looking up and down for any sign of injury. Which was ridiculous. Lexi hadn't even been inside. She was fine. Not hurt, not injured, perfectly fine.

"Our smoke alarm is going off. The guys went to check it out. I'm just thankful you're not in there. I couldn't see you with the others, I didn't know if..."

She trailed off, emotions clogging her throat and threatening to spill tears from her eyes. She caught Tommy exiting from the corner of her eye as Lexi mumbled, "Oh, shit."

He held up a half-burnt tea towel as the rest of the team filed out behind him. She turned back to Lexi, relief turning to confusion. Lexi's face was pale, except for the hint of pink getting redder on her cheeks.

"I'm so sorry."

Robyn frowned, her brain still trying to catch up with the ever-changing information and feelings. "Sorry for what?"

Lexi started to ramble then, her words spilling over each other to make their way out. "I put on eggs to boil and then realised we had no bread. So, I had to go to the store and get some. I thought they were off. I was sure I turned them off."

Robyn shook her head in disbelief as Tommy joined them, filling her in on what happened.

"Everything's fine, we got there right on time. The tea towel was thrown against the hob, it was only starting to singe when we got inside. The kitchen is full of smoke, but otherwise nothing was damaged. Well, apart from the eggs and this."

He passed a shell-shocked Lexi the tea towel.

"I've opened the windows up to air the place, but the rest of the building is good to go back in. I'm sure you'll hear it all from Red, but don't leave a cooker unattended. These things happen quicker than people expect."

He turned and started to pack up as Robyn stood there, staring at Lexi, the emotion that had ebbed at the sight of her flaring into anger. *These things happen quicker than people expect.* They were almost the exact words Robyn had used to explain to Lexi about the house fire that took her father's life. The memories of which were now slamming into the forefront of her mind with more force than they had in a long time.

"I can't—how could you be so careless?"

Robyn felt a prickle of remorse at the way Lexi's face fell, but this was too serious. It wasn't creating a mess around the place or forgetting to pick up after herself. This could have been far worse and endangered not only the residents of their building, but Robyn's team. Lexi started to apologise again and reached for Robyn, but Robyn pulled back and gathered her stuff.

"I've got to go. I've still got work to do. Don't go back into the apartment for a while. Even minor smoke inhalation can be serious. I'll check on the place after shift and message you."

At that, she turned and walked back to the truck, a mixture of anger, disappointment and embarrassment welling inside her. Hidden beneath it all, overwhelming fear waited, ready to consume her. The fire her father had died in was different in numerous ways, but right now it all felt the same. She glanced back around to see Lexi still standing where she'd left her, tears trailing down her cheeks with the bag presumably carrying the bread at her feet. Robyn ignored the twinge of regret she felt as she walked away from Lexi. She took her seat and avoided Tommy's gaze the whole way back to the station.

❖

Lexi's eyes burned from crying as she sat in her parents' kitchen. "You didn't see her face, Mom—she was so pissed."

Simone rubbed a soothing hand up and down Lexi's arm. "She was probably scared, honey. She thought you were in there."

Lexi shook her head, biting her lip to prevent more tears from falling. "No, after that. She was mad, disappointed. She called me careless, and she was right."

Simone didn't argue or refute Lexi's statement. She had always allowed Lexi to feel her feelings, and never minimised them. It was part of the reason why, for better or worse, Lexi still never hid them.

"You didn't mean for it to happen. But it could've been much worse, and Robyn knows that. She's seen much worse. It's not a vague potential in her mind, she's witnessed what it looks like."

Lexi considered how it must have been for Robyn. Being called to their address, not knowing if Lexi was safe, then hearing she had been the cause of it all to begin with.

"I'm just so mad at myself. I was sure I turned off the hob. Why didn't I check again?"

That was something she'd kick herself about for a long time coming.

"I know I can be forgetful, messy, flighty. But Robyn has drummed the fire safety stuff into me over and over. Not only did I leave the hob on, but I had to have flung that tea towel in its direction. I was distracted about the bread, because I had planned to make egg salad sandwiches and have them ready for later. Robyn loves egg salad sandwiches. I thought we could eat and talk and…" Her voice trailed off as she bit her lip anxiously.

"Talk about what?"

Lexi's eyes flitted up to Simone's knowing ones. She

hadn't spoken to her mom about anything that had transpired with Robyn yet. Not because she was unwilling to, simply because she hadn't visited since everything occurred. But with her emotions already at the surface, she spilled it all out right there on the table. She spoke about the car boot sale, her creative block, the fake date, their weekend together, albeit a tamer version, and everything that led up to the fire. Simone held her hand and nodded throughout, interjecting only to clarify a fact here or there, but otherwise letting her unload the whole thing.

"Everything was going so well. I was hoping the talk would be about things moving forward. I know Robyn has never been the relationship type, but things have just been so… different. She was letting me in. And then I did this." Lexi's voice cracked on the last word and she took a deep breath to contain the emotions bubbling up.

"It sounds like you two need to talk. Give her some time, she said she'd message you—so just take it slowly. She's probably going to be angry, and she gets to be. I know you didn't intend it, but it happened, so just let her feel it. But you remember what I told you about someone being angry with you."

Lexi nodded. "Even when someone is angry with me, I still deserve safety and respect."

Simone squeezed her hand as she parroted the words she had heard growing up. It had been a long time before she understood their importance. Not everyone learned at a young age that anger didn't mean someone got to treat you badly or withhold care. Lexi hadn't grown up in a house devoid of anger. But no matter what she did to deserve it, it never came with the punishment of losing her parents' love. It was a core value that had created a security she would forever be grateful for.

"Sam mentioned something and I've been thinking about it a lot, more so the past few hours since all of this happened."

Simone tilted her head at Lexi's words, and Lexi ploughed ahead, hoping someone else could help her make sense of her thoughts.

"You know she has ADHD. She mentioned that it can be genetic, and given Valerie's history, it's probable she inherited it from her. She spoke about a lot of things that I could relate to, like getting hyper-focused on something and losing track of time. When I was looking into it a little more, some things in my life started to make sense. But I don't know if that's because I'm just looking for an answer."

Lexi waited a moment as Simone looked thoughtful, then she nodded.

"That could make sense. There were some things growing up that had us wondering, but you were so passionate about your art and doing so well it was easy to brush it off."

Lexi was a little taken aback by that and grappled for a reply.

"What things? Wondering what?"

"You lost track of time a lot. Mostly when you were painting. Ever since you were a little kid, it was like you were in your own little creative world and nothing else existed. We were able to manage it by reminding you to take breaks to eat and get out of the house occasionally, although forcing you is likely a better word."

Simone laughed lightly and Lexi smiled, remembering the forced outings for fresh air all too well.

"We figured it was that amazing creative brain of yours taking over. But there were some other things in school. Your teacher recommended we get your ears tested not long after you started, because they were worried you couldn't hear properly. It would take a while to get your attention. We just put it down to daydreaming. You never struggled too much with schoolwork, so I guess it just didn't seem to bother you enough for us to look into more."

Memories flashed back then. Lexi recalled sitting in class at times, wondering how everyone else seemed to be able to pay attention and ask questions. Lexi survived on last minute cramming before any exams and promptly forgetting it all right after.

"So, you think it could be possible? That I might have ADHD like Sam?" Lexi asked.

"If any of these things are bothering you now, it's worth exploring at least. What's the worst that can happen, other than understanding yourself more? And your father and I will help as much as we can. Maybe we should've looked into things sooner, but there wasn't as much information about this stuff back then and you always seemed happy."

Lexi reached out and covered Simone's hand with hers.

"I was. I am. Even if I do have ADHD, I don't blame you guys for not knowing. You clearly helped me manage it well enough all along. Now I just need to figure out how to do that for myself."

Simone smiled before leaning in conspiratorially. "Now, tell me more about the fun parts. Do you love her?"

Lexi laughed, the knot in her chest easing slightly as it always did when she got things off her chest. "It's been a few days, Mom."

Simone raised an eyebrow and replied, "That's not what I asked."

Was she in love? Lexi thought about Robyn, her head filled with images of their times together. Not just the past couple of weeks, but before that. Their crime show binge-watching sessions, the inside jokes they'd created from years of cohabitation, the little things Robyn often did that made

Lexi's day better. Of course she loved Robyn, but was that the same as being in love? It was all so complicated, and not something she could figure out right now with the extra added emotions of the day.

She spent the rest of the afternoon at her parents', joining them for dinner when her dad returned from work. She allowed herself to be taken care of by them both, enjoying the care and affection she used to take for granted. Her dad gave her a stern lecture on fire safety, the fear evident on his face when she relayed the drama of the day. She lay on the couch after dinner, replaying it over and over in her head.

She thought again about what Sam and Simone had shared with her. Did she have ADHD? Could this be why these things happened? Nothing of this magnitude had ever occurred before, but it wasn't the first time her supposed carelessness had caused problems for her. Except *carelessness* didn't feel like the right word. It wasn't a lack of care—she didn't shrug her shoulders and decide not to check. So what was it, and how could she expect Robyn to understand when she didn't?

The day played like a movie on repeat. She had put the eggs in the pot and filled it with water. She had put the pot on the hob and turned it on. She had gotten out the salad bowl, mayonnaise, tomato, lettuce, and onion and started chopping. That's when she had glanced toward the empty bread bin. She had grabbed the tea towel to wipe her hands and walked to the cooker to turn off the hob. She obviously hadn't turned it off, and the tea towel had gotten abandoned there instead. She only knew that because it was the logical sequence of events, not because she remembered. *Why?*

She grabbed her phone to check if Robyn had messaged yet, and that's when it hit her. The action triggered a memory of her phone buzzing from the other side of the room. That had to be it. She had set down the tea towel and headed in search of her phone. She had intended to grab it and return to the hob. She remembered her heart flipping, hoping it was Robyn. It had just been a spam call, but it was enough to derail her from what she was supposed to be doing. She closed her eyes, guilt enveloping her completely. It *was* careless. Reckless. Dangerous.

The offending item pinged in her hand, and she opened her eyes, a mixture of emotions swirling when she saw Robyn's name lighting up her screen. One new message.

Apartment is clear. I'm going to crash at the station tonight, they needed someone to go on call, but you're free to go back. Talk tomorrow.

Lexi's heart sank. Robyn was avoiding her, and she couldn't blame her. She probably couldn't look at Lexi right now. A tear trailed down her cheek and she quickly swiped at it as her father walked into the room. He sat beside her with concern etched all over his face.

"You okay, Lexi Lou?"

She nodded, afraid to speak, then shook her head. Lying was pointless when she could already feel her tears starting again.

"How about you go get changed and stay here tonight? Your bed is always there, you know."

Lexi jumped at the offer, not yet ready to go back and face what she had done. Her empty apartment would make taking her mind off it all impossible. She changed into a set of pyjamas that she kept in her old room, which still housed her twin bed. The rest of the room contained plastic boxes. Photos, art, miscellaneous mementos. Her childhood all sealed up in neatly stacked and labelled containers. She spent some time looking through a box filled with her preschool paintings, and by the looks of it her parents hadn't gotten rid of any. The messy jumble of colours on thin copier paper brought back a happy memory.

Whether her father agreed with her career choice or not, Lexi couldn't deny that if he really wanted to stop her, he could have. He had always financially supported her dreams, even if it was begrudgingly. The neat handwriting on the newly labelled boxes was one she knew all too well. Her father was the one who did most of the organising in the house, always had been. So the fact that her art, going back to before she could even remember, was carefully stored spoke volumes.

She joined her parents in the living room as they were putting on a movie and grabbed a bowl of their freshly popped popcorn. Tomorrow she would need to untangle the mess that she had made, but tonight, she sank into familiar comforts surrounded by love.

CHAPTER FIFTEEN

Robyn paced back and forth after sending the message to Lexi to tell her the apartment was safe. She surveyed the kitchen. The burnt pot was in the sink, but apart from that, it was like nothing had happened. She took in the ingredients on the countertop from whatever Lexi had been preparing. It looked like egg salad, Robyn's favourite. Had Lexi been preparing it for her? She felt a soft ache inside, until she shut it down and began tidying. She put away everything except for the pot. She left that in the sink. Once the countertops were clear she grabbed a change of clothes and left, wanting to be out before Lexi returned.

Seeing Lexi would come with too many varied emotions. Robyn couldn't sort through them while anger was clouding her judgement. Lexi hadn't meant for it to happen. But regardless of intent, it had been such a reckless thing to do, and Robyn had seen all too often the damage that could have come from it. She lived with the grief that occurred from someone else's recklessness every day.

All her father's colleagues who'd regaled her with stories throughout the years focused on how much of a hero her father was. He had saved a little girl from that house fire and had made the team evacuate, and then gone back in to try to find her parents. When the fire was out, they found him inside the door with the woman next to him and an empty oxygen tank. The smoke inhalation had killed them both. Robyn was proud of him for his bravery, and always had been. But hero or not, her father was gone because of a series of preventable mistakes.

It was unfair to punish Lexi for a past that couldn't be changed, but Robyn couldn't help the comparisons her brain was drawing. She drove back toward the station and stopped, pulling into a parking spot next to Blaze. The on-call shift that night didn't require her being at the station for a couple of hours, so she had time, and right now she needed some familiarity. Old habits die hard. Robyn walked through the door of the establishment she knew so well and took in her surroundings. Her eyes landed on Freya standing at a table near the door. Robyn returned the nod Freya offered, then walked to the bar and ordered a soft drink. She couldn't drink alcohol while on call, but that hadn't been the point of her trip anyway.

She sensed more than saw the seat next to her become occupied and turned to take in the other woman. Freya looked good, and it seemed like she knew it. The last, and only, time they had hooked up had been with very little preamble. Robyn had gone to the bar looking for someone to get lost in, and Freya had made no attempt to play hard to get. They had spent an hour or so drinking and dancing, the friction and heat a form of foreplay more than anything. They had barely spoken the whole evening and had just allowed their eyes, hands, and lips to do most of the talking.

When they had gotten back to Robyn's apartment, they both knew what they wanted, and they took it. The sex had been hot and plentiful, but there was no emotion involved. A couple of hours later, when Freya had gotten up and put on her dress and heels without much conversation, Robyn was grateful. Passing out after sex was all well and good, until it led to the awkward next morning, and hoping the other person wouldn't want to stick around for breakfast or conversation. A quick goodbye and Freya had left—with no numbers exchanged or pretence about seeing each other again.

It wasn't lost on Robyn how different it had been when she'd woken up beside Lexi. It was surreal to consider that it had only been a day since that last occurred. She shook the image from her head and focused her attention on Freya, who had ordered another drink and was aiming a smile her way.

"I haven't seen you around much."

It was a statement rather than a question, so Robyn didn't feel the need to supply an answer. She nodded in acknowledgement and took a sip of her drink. Freya pointed toward it before asking, "Starting light?"

"I'm on call tonight, so no alcohol. I just stopped in for a while."

Freya angled herself toward Robyn, making sure her very generous cleavage was on full display. "Do you have enough time for a dance? Or we could get out of here and spend the time you have back at your place instead—it's pretty close if I remember."

Robyn stilled. The offer wasn't a surprise as such, but she had been so lost in her own head, she hadn't even considered how she would feel about it. One thing was for sure, regardless of the events of the day, there was no way she was bringing someone back to her place and running the risk of confronting Lexi with that.

"Can't, sorry. My place had a little smoke damage today, so it's airing out for the night."

Although it was partly true, Robyn wasn't sure why she had said it that way. She should have just turned Freya down rather than making up an excuse that left an opening, one that Freya jumped on immediately.

"No worries, my place isn't that far either if we grab a cab."

Freya was persistent, and Robyn considered it. What had happened between her and Lexi up until now felt important, but they hadn't made any commitments or even discussed doing so. Right now, it was all at the possibilities stage. A stage that seemed stalled after today. Robyn wouldn't be breaking any rules by going home with Freya and losing herself in a no-strings-attached hookup for a while. But relationship or not, the idea still knotted her stomach. It was something Robyn would have to unpack and sort through before she was available for anything or anyone, strings or not.

"Thanks for the offer, I'm just not in the place to accept right now. Don't get me wrong, I enjoyed our night together, so it has nothing to do with—"

Freya cut her off before she could continue. "Hey, it's fine. I know you did—trust me, I'm not concerned about that. If I was, I wouldn't have approached you. You looked like you could use some company, and we had amazing sex. But I'm not going to go and cry about the rejection, okay?"

Robyn smiled and nodded, wondering how everyone around her seemed so good at this whole open communication thing. Did she miss that lesson in school? There was no malice or hurt in Freya's voice, and it was clear she meant every word. She was already walking out the door with someone else before Robyn's glass was empty. Robyn did a double take as Freya held the door open for none other than Ollie, her new friendly neighbourhood nurse. Well, good for her. She couldn't help smiling to herself as she considered how the six degrees of lesbian separation was more like two degrees in their small town.

As she got to the station a little while later, she crashed in a bunk and willed sleep to come. It had been a long day and Robyn needed it to be over. The comfort and thrill she usually found at Blaze had gone, and now it left her feeling hollow. It wasn't difficult to figure out what changed. The bar had no hope of comparing to the comfort she'd found, however briefly, wrapped in Lexi's arms. Memories raced through her mind, all now clouded by a red haze of anger. Or, if she were being honest with herself, fear. Those few minutes where Robyn didn't know if Lexi was safe had fractured a part of her heart, the part that until recently had protective walls placed all around it. Robyn was angry, but mostly at herself for putting her heart back into the firing line. She needed to figure out how to return it to safety once more.

❖

Lexi entered her empty apartment the next day, still raw, but calmer from her night of childhood comforts. Robyn should still be on shift, so Lexi had planned to face the consequences of her actions without an audience. The minute she walked through the door and saw the burnt pot sitting in the sink, her gut clenched. It could have been so bad. She needed to find a way to ensure this didn't happen again. She walked to her room and dropped her stuff, picking up the carefully wrapped packages beside her wardrobe.

She was thankful that she had taken the time to wrap all the completed canvases the previous morning before the incident occurred. She gently unwrapped each one and they were the same as when she'd left them, no smoke damage, so that was at least one concern she could mark off her list. She still had the final piece to complete by the end of the week, and her motivation was currently at rock bottom again. Mostly from tiredness. She hadn't slept well the night before, even with the feeling of safety and comfort she felt in her old room. She'd had too much racing around her mind. She should try to get the piece done, but her bed was too inviting to ignore. She crawled beneath the covers and pulled them over her head, promising herself she'd work on the last piece after a quick nap. Painting required energy, right?

She didn't remember falling asleep, but she startled awake with a frantically beating heart from a nightmare that drifted from her memory before her eyes were even open. The room was dark despite the fact that she hadn't closed her curtains, so the power nap had extended for far longer than she'd intended. She checked the time on her phone and was shocked to realise it was after midnight. Sleep still clung to her like a wave threatening to pull her back under, but her throat ached for water the way it only ever did after a deep sleep.

She got up and tiptoed out of the room, worried about disturbing Robyn. Having been on call the night before, it meant Robyn worked back-to-back and would be exhausted. Not to mention the added stress Lexi had placed upon her. She glanced to the right at Robyn's open bedroom door. It was unusual for her to leave it ajar while sleeping, but the hopeful part of Lexi thought that maybe Robyn had wanted to see if she got up. Wishful thinking, but Lexi clung to it with everything she could muster.

She moved quietly toward the door, telling herself she would take a quick peek and leave Robyn be if she were sleeping. Despite Robyn's anger, and the guilt that weighed on Lexi, the ache she had to see Robyn outweighed her fear of confrontation. It wasn't like they could discuss all that had occurred this late anyway, they would need to wait to figure it all out. But just catching a glimpse of Robyn would go a long way to setting Lexi's world right side up again.

The empty bed beyond the door cut through Lexi deeper than it should have. The bed was still made exactly how Lexi herself had made it the morning of the fire, when Robyn left for work. That thought brought to mind waking up with Robyn, and the contentment at how right it all felt. Not to mention the shower that followed. Now here she was, alone in an empty apartment, with nobody to blame but herself.

Should she text Robyn and make sure she was safe? Would it be weird? It wasn't like Robyn had never spent the night elsewhere without informing Lexi before. But that had been different. *Hadn't it?* Lexi stopped short because ultimately, it hadn't. Robyn was an adult, and a free woman. She could be spending the night with someone else, forgetting all about the damage Lexi had caused.

It was like a sucker punch to the stomach and Lexi took a deep, steadying breath. She wasn't doing herself any favours with the self-inflicted guilt trip and intrusive images the thoughts conjured. Robyn could be staying at the station again. Or crashing with a friend. Worst-case scenarios wouldn't help anyone, but Lexi knew she was destined to run through them all once her head hit the pillow again, regardless.

She moved toward the fridge to grab water and stopped in her tracks, relief flooding her body as she almost laughed at the scene before her. A sleeping Robyn was curled up on the couch, book still precariously balanced in her grasp. Robyn was here. She was sleeping. How had Lexi missed that? Now that she was paying attention, the soft snores she had begun to love greeted her ears like a lullaby. She grabbed a blanket from the back of the chair and gently draped it over Robyn as she slept on. Her exhaustion was evident as she barely stirred while Lexi took her book and laid it on the coffee table.

After grabbing the water she had come in search of, Lexi retreated to her room and got back under the covers. She had been tempted to curl up right there with Robyn, and the night before she wouldn't have hesitated to do so. But right now, with things as they were, she wasn't willing to push any boundaries. She would take the win that Robyn was home and succumb to the sleep she still desperately needed, her heart and head both in a significantly brighter place than before.

CHAPTER SIXTEEN

The sweet smell of pancakes was the first thing to awaken Robyn's senses, closely followed by a humming she knew only too well. She felt a moment of quiet happiness before memories came flooding back. Her gut clenched as she recalled the almost-fire and the fact that she was still irate. Even pancakes couldn't fix that, extra toppings and all. She lay on the couch for a moment, trying to figure out how this morning would go. What she should say, how things would be, whether Lexi would address it or pretend like nothing happened. Or worse, brush it off as if it wasn't a big deal.

"I know you're awake," Lexi said.

Robyn stilled, then sat up reluctantly. "How could you possibly have known that?"

Lexi's hair was thrown up in a messy bun. Her legs were on display in the cotton shorts she sported and Robyn's gaze immediately fell to her ass. Robyn sighed in frustration. She was trying to maintain her momentum of annoyance—couldn't Lexi just roll with it and look less than perfect for one damn morning?

"Because you stopped snoring."

Robyn huffed and replied in a petulant tone, "I do not snore."

"Do too. How else would I know you were awake? Don't worry, it's a cute little snore, not a loud obnoxious one."

"I. Do. Not. Snore. And I definitely do not *cutely* snore."

Lexi chuckled, turning to look at Robyn as she cocked an eyebrow. "Oh, yes, sure, it's a strong, warrior-like snore. Super loud and terrifying to all that dare enter your lair as you slumber."

Robyn frowned and shook her head in exasperation. It was less because of Lexi's teasing, and more because Lexi was making it very difficult to stay angry. "You're impossible, Sunny."

The soft upturn of Lexi's mouth at the nickname tugged at Robyn's heart.

"I'm sorry, Robs," Lexi whispered. The quiet words were accompanied by tear-filled eyes that Lexi quickly tried to hide.

She hated seeing Lexi so unsure, even if there were valid reasons behind the uncertainty between them. Lexi turned back to the cooker, taking the food up and subtly swiping at her cheeks. Robyn wanted to go to Lexi and console her, but she wasn't quite ready for that yet. She gave Lexi the time to compose herself by going to get changed. She made sure to let Lexi know she'd be back for breakfast so they could talk. Anger or not, she wouldn't walk out of the room when Lexi was clearly making an effort. Plus, she saw chocolate chips in the batter.

After freshening up, she joined Lexi at the table. The food looked as good as it smelled, but Lexi seemed on edge. Her gaze kept moving around the room and she chewed her bottom lip more than the food on her plate. After Lexi got up a second time during the first five minutes, Robyn followed her movements to see Lexi checking the cooker switch. The third time Lexi made to leave her seat, Robyn covered her hand to stop the action.

"It's off, Lex. I can see it from here."

Lexi nodded, but her eyes kept darting toward the kitchen.

"You've checked it twice. I can see it. It's off. You can't keep checking or you'll never stop."

Robyn's hand was still covering Lexi's, the soft skin beneath her palm so familiar. Once Lexi settled back into her seat, she pulled her hand back to pick up her fork and continue eating.

"I'm so sorry. I know that doesn't change anything, but I'm going to prove it to you. I promise I'll make sure nothing like this happens again."

Robyn nodded, unsure of what to reply. They needed to talk more, but what would she say? She wasn't quite ready to absolve Lexi, but she hated being the cause of her uneasiness. And Lexi was clearly being harder on herself than Robyn could or wanted to be. The anger was dissipating, but the fear lodged in her chest still remained.

"I know you are. I just…it could've been so bad. I know you know that, so I'm not trying to guilt trip you. I just can't get past those thoughts right now, you know?"

Lexi nodded. Her shoulders slumped at Robyn's words. "Yeah, I understand. I could've destroyed everything. You work hard for what you've got, and it all could have been gone in minutes. Because of my carelessness."

A frown formed on Robyn's face as she replayed the words in her head. "You think I'm angry because my stuff might've gotten ruined?"

Lexi shrugged, followed by a sigh. "Well, no. Not exactly. I know how important fire safety is to you, and there's a lot of other people in these apartments that were affected by my actions. But yeah, your stuff is also important. I know everyone says shit like things are replaceable. But you've got memories and important irreplaceable items here."

Robyn sat back in her seat, pancakes forgotten. The anger resurfaced and mixed with the fear that hadn't budged, causing a volcano of words that she tried to hold back.

"You really have no idea, do you?" Robyn's tone was clipped, and Lexi flinched. She opened and closed her mouth but didn't get a word out, because Robyn couldn't contain the eruption of her own.

"I couldn't give a fuck about my stuff, Lexi. Everyone says things are replaceable because *they are*. You know what's not replaceable? *You*. Of course I care about the other people in these apartments, but there was only one person I stood down there looking for. I searched for a glimpse of your face just to get my heart to beat again."

Robyn's breathing was laboured, and she knew this wasn't productive. But her usual method of shutting down her emotions hadn't worked, so they had nowhere to go but out.

"I almost defied my boss's orders to go in there and find you, something I would never have done before. For a few minutes that felt like a lifetime, I pictured you trapped up there, alone, scared, hoping I would save you, while I had to stand there and watch. It's been a very long time since I've been as helpless, as terrified, as I was at that moment. So no, I did not care about losing my *stuff*, Lexi. I cared about losing you."

Tears streamed freely down Lexi's face as Robyn finished. She took a deep, steadying breath, but her fight or flight mode was well and truly activated. This was too much. The fear engulfed her, memories raced around her head of panic and helplessness from the day before, and from a day twenty years ago. It all blurred together as one until Robyn stood. Her brain wrestled with the part of her that badly wanted to rush to Lexi and wrap her arms around her until the tears subsided.

"Robyn." The cracked, whispered word was like a dagger, slicing at her reserve.

Robyn willed her feet to move, to fix this, to find safety once more. But none of this was safe. She took a step back, then another, before choking out her own quiet, broken words.

"I can't."

She turned to mask the onslaught of emotion that overwhelmed her as she fled to the safety of her room. She curled on her bed in the exact same position she had done as a twelve-year-old girl, grieving for the loss of her father, her life, and of love as she had known it. Love she had been running from ever since.

❖

What just happened?

Lexi had been staring at the closed door of Robyn's bedroom, that one thought circling her mind as the remainder of their food went cold. The onslaught of overwhelming feelings was difficult to untangle. She had been prepared for Robyn's anger, her disappointment, her annoyance. But what she hadn't been prepared for was the raw fear that radiated from every word. Because of her. Robyn was afraid to lose her.

It was silly to be shocked by that. She was important to Robyn, she knew that. Not because they slept together—long before it. This felt different, though. Like the thought of losing her was too hard for Robyn to comprehend. A secret, selfish part of Lexi couldn't help feeling good about how much Robyn cared. Maybe once she had calmed down, they could talk about what it all meant for them.

"If she calms down," Lexi mumbled to herself, finally unsticking herself from the chair to tidy off the uneaten food. She set up the easel then, planning to finish off the last piece to get it done with. Disappointment washed over her before the paintbrush was even in her hand because it wasn't going to happen. Her motivation was still elusive, and she couldn't figure out how to get it back. There was no secret formula that made it appear last time, but she needed to try something. She closed her eyes and thought back to the morning she had woken, ready to kick herself into gear and get it done. What had motivated her then?

Robyn.

She rolled her eyes internally at herself. What was she, a lovesick teenager who relied on a romantic muse to create art? It was preposterous. Lexi had been painting far longer than she had been crushing on Robyn; the two were not connected. But the more she really considered it, she couldn't deny that creating something she didn't feel passionate about had been easier when there were other forms of passion in her life. Those other forms of passion happened to come in the shape of her tall, dark, and gorgeous roommate.

With things so precarious between her and Robyn, she couldn't rely on that as motivation. No matter how things progressed, she never wanted her creativity to be dependent on another person. She needed to figure out how it all worked, and she had a feeling Sam was the one to help her with that. She shot off a quick text to see if Sam was free, and they made plans to meet at Blaze when it opened for lunch. It was close to Sam and Brooke's place, so worked as a good meeting spot. Lexi had offered to come to their house, but it seemed like Sam needed the time out too.

Robyn didn't emerge from her room for the few hours before she left to meet Sam. Lexi wrote a quick note to let her know where she was. It was probably unnecessary, but it was Lexi's compromise to stop herself from using her departure as an excuse to knock on Robyn's door and tell her in person. She hopped on the bus and spent the ride ruminating over everything. Part of her still worried about overreacting and jumping to conclusions. Everyone dealt with creative blocks at times, right?

But it wasn't just about that, and she knew it. Lexi had promised Robyn she would make sure something like the fire wouldn't happen again. But had that been realistic? How could she stick to her promise if she didn't even fully understand how or why it happened in the first place? Everything kept coming back in her head to the things Sam had told her. Could she have ADHD, like Sam mentioned? Lexi had nothing to lose by talking to her sister and at least learning as much as she could. Knowledge was power, or so she hoped.

Sam was already waiting in a booth when Lexi walked through the door. The place was quieter than she'd ever seen, but then again Lexi had only ever been there at night. The first time she had come was not long after she moved in with Robyn. Robyn had invited her when she mentioned going out. It was the first and certainly not the last time Lexi had gotten to see Robyn work her magic.

It was funny to think that she could have been here at the same time as her sister before they had ever even met. Although they looked so alike it probably would've been obvious had they unknowingly crossed paths. She slid across from Sam in the booth and took in the dark circles under her eyes.

"You look like death warmed up."

Sam groaned at her words, head falling into her hands. "I am so tired."

She patted Sam's head gently before asking, "Aren't the sleepless nights supposed to start *after* the baby arrives?"

Sam raised her head again, the tiredness not detracting from the glow that lit her eyes every time someone mentioned the baby's impending arrival.

"Brooke's still getting a lot of the not-so-morning sickness.

Then on top of it, Finley stopped sleeping through the night for the first time in his life. I swear that kid was barely a few months old when he started sleeping till morning. Now he's six, and when we should be saving up sleep before a newborn arrives, he's deciding to give us some late-night practice."

Lexi squeezed Sam's hand and smiled in sympathy. "Do you think it's because of the baby coming?"

Sam shrugged, muffling a yawn. "Your guess is as good as mine. He seems excited about it, but it has to be on his mind. He's had his mom and me all to himself for six years, it'll be an adjustment. I just never anticipated that adjustment starting before the baby was here. Obviously, I want to let Brooke rest as much as possible, so I've been listening out for him before he disturbs her, which means I'm not sleeping well even when he doesn't wake."

Lexi knew she had nothing in the way of advice to offer but wanted to be supportive. She was already formulating a plan to kidnap her nephew for some bonding time that would let his moms get some sleep in the process.

"Now's probably not the time for me to lay all my drama on you, then."

Sam shook her head vehemently at Lexi's words. "No, no. I need the drama. My life is all baby planning, a puking wife, and sleepless nights right now, your drama is free dopamine. Let's order food and then you can regale me with life outside of parenthood."

Lexi laughed and went to place their order. As much as Sam grumbled, Lexi knew she loved it. Sam's life was far from perfect, and her path to this point had been filled with far more twists and turns than Lexi could imagine. But she was happy. Exhausted, but happy. While waiting for the food to arrive, Lexi filled Sam in on the fire incident. Sam was concerned but understanding. She spoke about similar incidents that had happened to her over the years and simply hearing her speak about them without hesitance or shame made Lexi feel a little better than before.

"I've been thinking more about the things you talked about. I've tried to do some research on ADHD and a lot makes sense, but it's so hard to sort through it all."

Sam nodded. "It can be overwhelming. But I'm happy to help as much as I can. What kind of things stood out?"

"I spoke to my mom after the fire, and I mentioned ADHD. She brought up some things from childhood that stood out to her. It resurfaced some memories for me too. Like feeling so embarrassed when the teacher would call on me and I couldn't even remember hearing her ask a question. That sounds silly but it happened so often."

Much like her parents, Lexi had always put her distractedness down to being creative, an artist. Nothing mattered more than that, so she didn't pay attention. She never really considered that she *couldn't*.

"I always figured that I just wasn't trying hard enough, and my parents never pushed too much because my school reports were never bad."

"That's more common than you'd think. It's one of the reasons ADHD is so underdiagnosed in women. Society expects us to act in certain ways, and so girls are far more likely to conform to those expectations, even if it takes so much more energy to do that."

Their food arrived and they began to eat as Lexi considered Sam's words.

"Now that I'm thinking about it, there are all these little things that never seemed to add up to anything until suddenly now, they do. I guess with art and my parents support I've just always been able to manage it. But now it all feels like it's spinning out of control and I'm not sure how to manage anything anymore."

Sam nodded, allowing Lexi space to get it all out.

"I'm worried about going down the wrong track. Like I'm just trying to find an excuse for all of this and trying to make the pieces fit—"

Sam held her hands up, cutting Lexi off. "If the pieces fit, they fit. If some pieces fit, and others don't, that's also okay. We are not puzzles. ADHD isn't a jigsaw you need to hold every piece of to make it real, no matter what anyone tries to tell you."

Sam's passion was clear as she spoke, frustration evident in her voice. Lexi understood it wasn't aimed at her.

"So, what do I do now? I need to get this commission done. And I was so happy to get most of it out of the way. I can't fall at the last hurdle. I need this, Sam, for more than just the money. And even if I do finish it, what then? The thoughts of doing this over and over are almost as scary as never doing it at all."

"Obviously, what works for me is highly dependent on the fact that I take medication to help with ADHD," Sam said.

"So, is medication necessary? Will it be like this unless I figure that side out?"

Sam took a sip of her drink before replying.

"I wouldn't say necessary, because like I said, no two people with ADHD are the same. Medication is an important and powerful support and unfortunately can be highly stigmatized. Being properly medicated for my ADHD changed my life. But I also know many people in my support group who thrive without medication and have found things that work for them."

"There's a support group?" Lexi asked, her interest piqued.

"Yep. There's a lot of them. You can even do them virtually now. Mine is an established group, so honestly a lot of the time we just chat and help each other get stuff done. Body doubling, like I mentioned before. I'll send you some information on the support groups for people getting information. It's a good starting point."

Lexi nodded, grateful to have Sam help her sift through the overwhelming amount of information.

"But the most important thing, Lex—stop with the self-blame spiral. You will find what works for you with your art. You may need to try a lot until then. The worst thing you can do is get mad at yourself every time you struggle. You got this far without it being as much of a problem because you've been nurtured and loved and cared for. Now you need to do the same for yourself. You deserve that."

Lexi smiled, her heart warming at the words. The conversation and validation she received from Sam already had her feeling more confident about going in the right direction with what she had to do.

"I struggle a lot with the paperwork side of things. I know there are grants and scholarships and residencies for artists. There's a lot of support if you know where to find it, but I feel like it's all stuck behind mountains of paperwork I never seem to be able to finish. I know having access to the financial support would give me the space to really figure out my direction as an artist, instead of scrambling to make money from art and zapping my desire in the process."

Sam nodded and pulled her legs up beneath her as she replied. "That all makes sense. A lot of these supports are hard to access, especially for neurodivergent people. So much of the world is. Typically, people who design these support systems don't consider the barriers they are creating with the number of steps it takes someone to even start the process. Each of those steps is a chance to forget or get distracted or get overwhelmed. But that's where you need to reach out, lean on the many people in your corner. What about Dani? She's volunteered at the community centre for years with the young artist groups. I bet she's done this a lot."

Lexi had been avoiding Dani a little bit. Not consciously, but she knew it had been a while since she reached out. Longer than normal.

"I think I feel a little ashamed. Embarrassed. Dani worked so hard to help me get these commissions. And I feel like it will seem like I'm ungrateful and whining. I should be happy with how lucky I am to have so much support, you know?"

Sam reached across the table and pulled Lexi's hand into hers. "This is what I mean. This shame is not going to get you anywhere good. You need to stop expecting yourself to just be able to do it, you'll keep hitting a brick wall with that one. Accept that right now you need help and ask for it. Dani is never going to think less of you for that. Anyone who would doesn't deserve an opinion."

Lexi promised to reach out to Dani as they started getting ready to leave. "As payment for listening to my mess, you're going to book a night away with Brooke soon and I'm going to get some well needed bonding time with my nephew. Promise me?"

Sam's eyes lit up at the offer and she pulled Lexi into a tight hug. "I'm not even going to pretend to protest. I need some time with my wife before the next one gets here and they gang up on us."

Lexi laughed as they headed toward the exit, happy to be able to do something practical to help. She was lost in thoughts of things she planned to try once she got home, invigorated by Sam's advice and empathy, and ready to tackle the final piece. She was so caught up in her daydreams as she exited the building that she nearly barrelled through someone about to walk through the door.

"Shit, sorry, I didn't see you there." Her eyes landed on a familiar face, but she struggled to place her.

The woman shot her a smile as recognition flashed across her face. "Robyn's, right?"

Lexi frowned, then a lightbulb went off. She was the last woman who'd left Robyn's room—it seemed like a lifetime ago, though it occurred to Lexi that it was only a few weeks.

"Oh, yeah, I'm Robyn's...roommate. Lexi."

The woman nodded, her smile never wavering. She was even more beautiful up close and personal than she had been walking out of their apartment that night.

"Freya, nice to meet you. Is the apartment okay?"

Freya. That was it. The name hadn't been coming to her. Lexi was trying to catch up to the conversation and stop her head from making comparisons that wouldn't help anyone. "Uh, apartment?"

She was speaking in words rather than sentences which didn't add to the insecurities swirling around her mind, but she was confused about the context of the question.

"Robyn mentioned about the smoke damage when we met the other night. I'm glad it's all okay, then," Freya said.

Lexi's stomach plummeted as she sidestepped a couple making their way to the entrance. Freya shot her a wave and ventured inside behind them, leaving Lexi standing in the late afternoon sun that did little to warm the ice-cold chill that had suddenly descended upon her.

CHAPTER SEVENTEEN

R obyn paused the show she had been mindlessly staring at on her TV at the sound of the door closing. After venturing out in search of snacks earlier, she had seen Lexi's note saying she was going to meet Sam and would be back later. Robyn had taken the time to try to unwind and sort through the feelings, both old and new, that were hovering at the surface. Her instincts yelled at her to push them back down, but if there was any hope of moving past this, they needed to be acknowledged.

Part of that was acknowledging that she had feelings for Lexi that extended beyond a simple crush. It had been obvious for a while now, but coming right out and saying it, if only to herself, was a big step for Robyn. Those feelings were the true catalyst of the fear that led to her outburst. The fire had just brought it all to the surface. The thing she needed to figure out was if she could move past that fear and see where things could go with Lexi.

One thing Robyn understood in the hours she'd spent contemplating everything was that losing Lexi was terrifying. But it was already terrifying, regardless of what direction their relationship moved. Would it have hurt any less to find out Lexi was in that fire if they hadn't slept together? Things certainly felt different now, but it's not like they could rewind the clock and go back to how it used to be. She needed to figure out what she wanted before anything else happened, because Lexi deserved more than her uncertainty. And, Robyn acknowledged, so did she.

She pulled herself up from her bed and walked into the living room, where Lexi's back was to her as she stood at her easel. She coughed a little so as not to startle Lexi before speaking. "Can we talk?"

The words echoed loudly in the silence of the room, a silence that stretched on for longer than was comfortable before Lexi finally replied.

"I can't. I need to get this done. It's due tomorrow."

That wasn't the response Robyn had anticipated, but it was fair. Robyn couldn't simply demand a conversation whenever it suited her. Lexi went about busying herself with setting up her paint palette and Robyn regrouped before trying again.

"How about later when you're done? Or tomorrow? I'm off work," Robyn said.

Lexi didn't even turn around and Robyn got a bad feeling.

"I'm not sure how long this will take. It hasn't been going well. I'll let you know. You should probably tell your mom I'm not around for dinner tomorrow, though."

Robyn had completely forgotten about dinner with the chaos of the week. She was about to reply when Lexi continued in a tone that held far more bite than before, "Maybe you can take Freya instead."

Robyn was taken aback by the words and Lexi's demeanour. *Freya? Where does she come into all of this?* Robyn wasn't sure she could remember Lexi ever sounding so cold before. Even when she was struggling with painting, she had never shut Robyn out.

"I'm confused. Freya?" Robyn replied.

"I really need space to work right now. The studio is closed but I can take this into my room if you want the living room."

This wasn't Lexi. Something was very wrong. Robyn stood, uncertain whether to push further, but not feeling sure enough about anything to do so. Instead, she spoke softly, leaving the ball in Lexi's court.

"You stay. I can go to my room. Just knock if you feel like talking, though. I'd really like to figure this out. All of it."

Lexi didn't reply, but Robyn caught the soft sigh that emanated from her before she picked up a paintbrush and started to work. Robyn retreated back to the safety of her bedroom, wishing she had never left it.

❖

The following evening, she was seated across from her mom at a table in the same restaurant where they held her sister's anniversary party. She waited for the inevitable barrage of questions, still uncertain how she would answer them.

"Why did you say Lexi couldn't make it again? A deadline?"

Robyn nodded, but something inside her shifted. Appeasing her mother, lying for her approval was no longer a top priority. It was fitting that the lie should end in the same place it had begun.

"We're not dating."

Her mom's frown, which usually would have had Robyn's stomach clenching, no longer had the same effect.

"You broke up? Already?"

Before she could stop herself, the words escaped her lips in a sea of honesty. Lexi had broken something inside her, but not necessarily for the worse. She had taken apart the walls Robyn erected piece by piece, by showing her that sometimes honesty was a lot easier than these games people played. Robyn included.

A wide range of emotions flitted across her mother's features as Robyn relayed the fake date scenario, even following up with the actual feelings she harboured and the fear that was holding her back. It was like a lid lifting on Pandora's box, and Robyn couldn't stop it if she tried. The last thing she was expecting was the warm, comforting hand that her mother reached across the table to cover her own.

"Robyn. Why didn't you just talk to me?"

Robyn bit back a snort. There was only so far her honesty would go unless she found a way to sugarcoat it. "I didn't want to disappoint you again."

"My baby. You have no idea how proud I am of you, do you?"

Robyn wanted to believe it, to take comfort and hope from the words. But frustration won over and she couldn't ignore reality.

"How would I possibly know that? When have you ever told me that? All I hear is how I need to settle down, how disappointed you are every time I come to an event solo. You act like my life has no meaning, Mom. Like I need to find love to be complete. But look at what love did to you."

She wanted to snatch back the last words the minute they left her mouth, but she couldn't. She dropped her head, unable to look her mom in the eye. "I'm sorry, I didn't mean that."

"You did, but you're wrong. I'm the one who's sorry. I guess I haven't actually told you how proud I am. For much the same reason you're sitting here alone with me tonight. Fear."

Robyn lifted her head and frowned as her mother continued.

"You are your father's daughter, Robyn. That's the highest compliment I could ever pay you, because I loved that man with every fibre of my being. You're right, I want you to find someone and settle down. Not because I think your life is worthless otherwise. But because I know what it's like to love and be loved so fiercely. It's the best feeling in the whole world, my darling. How could I not want my children to experience that?" Tears glistened in the corner of her mother's eyes.

"But you lost Dad, and I saw the pain you went through. That you still go through."

Her mom shook her head and squeezed Robyn's hand tightly. "You say I don't see you, Robyn, but you don't see me either. You look at me and you see the broken woman I was after your father's death. And I admit I was broken. Of course I was, I lost the only future I had imagined."

Her mom's hand began to shake slightly on top of hers and Robyn moved to cover it with her other hand, holding tightly. Her mom smiled as she composed herself and continued.

"You withdrew after your dad died. You became so distant and I had no idea how to reach you, and honestly, I didn't have the energy to figure it out until suddenly it was too late. I'm sorry for that. I should have tried harder. Your father always knew the right thing to say, he never had to try hard to bring a smile to your face. And then suddenly you were left with just me and it didn't feel like enough. I didn't feel like enough for you."

Robyn's throat ached from unshed tears as she listened to her mom. It hit her that although they had lived through something monumental together, it didn't mean they lived through it in the same way.

"But I'm not in pain, baby. I miss your dad every day and I always will, but I wouldn't trade a second of the time we had together because of it. Losing your father was the worst thing that ever happened to me. But loving him gave me many of the best things, including you and your sisters, and my wonderful grandkids. Your dad gave me a lifetime of love, even if he's not here to share it."

The way her mother spoke about things was so far from the image in Robyn's head that it had her reeling. Was it true? Had Robyn seen what she expected rather than what was real? It would take a lot more than this conversation to work through it all, but it was almost like seeing a glimpse of the mother she used to know, someone she thought was lost forever. Now it seemed like maybe they were finally seeing the path that could lead them back to each other.

"I want to say it clearly now. I am so very proud of the woman you've become, Robyn. Your father is too, I know that without a doubt."

Robyn's cheeks were wet from the tears she no longer held back.

"I'm not going to pretend this is the career I would have chosen for you. It terrifies me, the thought of losing you like we did your dad. But I can see how much you love it, and from what I hear, you are very good at what you do."

"What you hear?" Robyn asked.

"You don't think I check up on you? Some people have been at that station longer than you've been alive, my dear."

Robyn laughed at the playful glint in her mother's eye. It warmed her to know that her mom had been interested in Robyn's career enough to check up on her.

They spent the rest of the meal having some of the most honest conversations Robyn could remember. When they touched back on the conversation about Lexi, her mom took both of Robyn's hands in hers and said the one thing that set everything in perspective.

"You'd better not let your dad's death be the thing that

keeps you from finding the love he always wished for you. Because that, my darling, is the last thing he would want his legacy to be."

❖

Lexi had dropped off the art pieces at the office, right on schedule, and the relief was immense. She wasn't winning any awards for the work, but the company purchaser had been happy, and she was proud of herself for getting it done. It had taken her until this afternoon to finalise the last piece, using a variety of the tips Sam had sent her after their lunch. The majority of the fuel she needed came from trying to block out the memory of Freya's words.

When we were together.

Robyn had been with Freya the night of the fire. It was the only timeline that made sense, considering she was home Wednesday night. Lexi remembered the panic, followed by the relief she had felt upon seeing Robyn asleep on the sofa. It had never entered her head that maybe Robyn had been with someone else the night before. *On-call, my ass.* Lexi wasn't sure if she was more pissed at the fact that Robyn had lied, or the fact that Robyn had jumped into bed with someone else the minute Lexi screwed up. Okay, it was definitely the latter part. But it was childish of her to avoid Robyn, even if she did have a very legitimate reason.

Her go-to had always been talking it through, honesty, and straightforward communication. She hated when people fell out over silly miscommunications because one or both refused to have an actual conversation. But she was human, and right now she was hurt. Robyn hadn't cheated on her, there was no relationship to cheat on. But it still ached like a betrayal.

Her phone rang in her pocket and her heart betrayed her

too by hoping against her will that it would be Robyn on the other end. When Dani's name flashed up, she smiled and answered the call.

"You did it!"

Dani had been the second person she texted, after Sam, when she completed the last piece. She had been integral to Lexi getting the job in the first place, and Lexi wanted to share the updates with her.

"I did. Finally."

"You did it. That's what matters. Are you celebrating?"

Lexi shrugged, then remembered Dani couldn't see her from the other end of the phone.

"Does wandering around the city lost in my thoughts count as celebrating?" Lexi replied.

"It does not. Come to Blaze, I'm here already with Ollie. I'll ask Sam and Brooke to join us. Brooke just told me Finley's grandparents offered to take him tonight, so they'll be kid free. You should invite Robyn too. You need to celebrate."

Lexi considered her options. Going home to her bed wasn't as tempting as it would have been a week ago. She needed company to shut her brain off. "Robyn's at dinner with her mom tonight. But that sounds good. See you there in thirty minutes?"

She ended the call after further confirmation and walked in the direction of the bar. Twice in a week would be a first for her, but Dani was right. She needed to celebrate this. Regardless of everything else, this week had been a breakthrough for Lexi in understanding more about herself and how to be her own muse when she needed it. That was an important achievement.

She walked through the doors to see Dani and who she presumed to be Ollie at the table to the right. Dani aimed a big smile at Lexi and pulled her into a hug as Lexi joined her.

"I am so frickin' proud of you."

Lexi pulled back and wiped a stray tear from her eye. "Stop. You're making me cry already. You'd swear I hadn't just done my job."

Sam and Brooke joined them at that moment and Sam shook her head, pointing her finger at Lexi. "Don't you go minimizing. This is a big deal, let us celebrate it. We are all proud of you."

As Dani took care of introductions between them all and Ollie, Lexi's heart squeezed tight at the smiling faces around her. The people who had supported her to get here. A pang of sadness hit at the notable absence of one of her biggest recent supporters.

"So, what made it happen? Did you try any of the stuff we discussed?"

Lexi shook Robyn from her thoughts as she focused her attention on Sam. "Yeah, I did. Some of it helped. Most of it just got me to start, which has been the hardest part. Once I started, it came more easily."

Lexi didn't mention the fact that the thing that worked best was trying to quell the bubbling emotions at the thought of Robyn with Freya. Might not be the healthiest of methods, but passion was passion. Even if it came steeped in anger. Despite that, Lexi still wished Robyn were here with her celebrating. *Damn it.*

"So, Dani, has this been going on long?"

Lexi perked up as Brooke pointed between Dani and Ollie. Dani shook her head, talking loudly over the music.

"Ollie is just a friend. We've been friends since we were kids. She moved here a few months ago."

Sam sighed in relief and her face went red as all eyes turned to her. She blurted out sheepishly, "Nothing against you or anything, Ollie, but Dani and Ruby are totally endgame."

"Ruby left, so you may want to update your game plan."

Dani mumbled as Ollie laughed good-naturedly, nodding in agreement.

Brooke waved a hand, clearly not accepting Dani's response. "She'll be back. Have you seen you? But I'm glad you're back out and about. I was worried for a while."

Dani smiled, but her face said she'd rather be talking about anything else.

"Let's talk about someone else's love life, shall we? Ollie has jumped back into the dating scene this week." Dani chuckled as all eyes swivelled to Ollie.

Sam was the first to speak. "We need details. You don't understand how little gossip there is around here lately. The highlight of most of my days are new baby clothes and sleep. So, spill."

Lexi couldn't help laughing at her sister as Ollie shrugged her shoulders lightly.

"I'm not sure there's much to tell. We slept together once, that's all. Dating is a stretch."

That didn't deter Sam. "Are you seeing her again? *Oh,* is she here?"

Sam's head swivelled as if the mystery woman would appear before them. Ollie and Lexi both laughed.

"I haven't seen her tonight. And I doubt it, I'm pretty sure she's a love 'em and leave 'em type, which is fine."

Ollie had a twinkle in her eye, a sign that the encounter had been a memorable one. "It's not usually my style, but my ex finally updated her relationship status on social media to single Tuesday night, so I was in a mood. Her name is Freya and she's an expert with her tongue, but I can't tell you much more than that."

Brooke and Sam both laughed at Ollie's candid remarks, but Lexi froze. That damn name again.

"Wait, did you say Tuesday night?" Lexi asked.

Freya wasn't that unusual a name, but combined with the day, it was all a little too coincidental.

"Yeah, Tuesday. We met here, actually," Ollie replied.

That had to be more than a coincidence. Lexi couldn't help it, she needed to know.

"Tall, long blond hair, legs for days?"

Ollie's expression was puzzled as she replied. "I guess you've met Freya before? Her legs are definitely a standout feature."

Lexi was shaking her head now, trying to make it make sense. *So, what, Freya slept with Ollie and then Robyn, or the other way around?*

"Freya told me she was with Robyn Tuesday night."

Even saying the words sent a shiver through Lexi, and not the good kind. A look of concern moved across both Brooke's and Sam's faces at the same time.

"You remember Robyn, the firefighter? She's Lexi's… roommate," Dani supplied to a confused Ollie. Lexi didn't miss the hesitation before the word *roommate*.

"That's weird. She definitely said they were together? I mean, she spoke to Robyn. I saw them chatting at the bar. That's how we got talking, actually," Ollie said.

Dani interjected, looking like a lightbulb went off for her.

"*Oh*, Freya. That's the blond goddess who approached Robyn the night we were here. I was surprised Robyn shot her down so quickly. But if I remember correctly, Robyn was far more interested in heading home."

Dani gave Lexi a knowing look before Ollie continued.

"Honestly, I was just looking for an excuse to talk to Freya. She looked like exactly the distraction I needed. So I asked how she knew Robyn. I explained I was new in town and a nurse over at the hospital, so I'd only recently placed Robyn's face when she came into the hospital."

Ollie's cheeks started to turn a shade of pink as she added the next part with a shrug. "She joked about how Robyn had shot her down for the second time, then asked if I wanted to take her place. It was a terrible pick-up line, but I was fine with being her back-up to get my mind off my ex."

Ollie picked up her drink as Lexi placed hers down, realisation dawning that she had gotten it all wrong. So very wrong. She was a prime culprit of the thing she'd only recently claimed to hate: miscommunication. She closed her eyes, remembering the line she had shot at Robyn in anger.

Maybe you can take Freya instead.

Lexi had been so wrapped up in everything going on for her with her art, the fire, and the thoughts about ADHD that she had assumed the worst about Robyn. Something Robyn had given Lexi no reason to believe. Why had she been so quick to think Robyn would go sleep with someone else at the first bump in the road? That was something she needed to figure out because Robyn deserved an answer. That is, if she was even willing to hear Lexi out after the way she'd been acting.

Lexi stood up and excused herself to go.

"You sure you're okay?" Sam rounded the table to pull her close.

"Yeah. I just have some making up to do. I jumped to the wrong conclusions and may have been a bit of an ass."

"Change into a low-cut top. It always gets me out of trouble," Sam stage-whispered.

Brooke swatted at Sam's ass, mumbling, "I heard that."

Lexi laughed and Sam squeezed her tight before letting her go once she promised to get a taxi home right outside. Now she had to hope she wasn't too late to fix this new mess and work on making less of them going forward. Or at the very least, ones that were far more fun.

CHAPTER EIGHTEEN

It was late when Robyn departed her childhood home. She had brought her mom there after dinner and been talked into a cup of tea before the drive back to her apartment. Her mom still lived in the same small town she'd grown up in. It wasn't quite rural, but it was far enough out of the city that the dark sky was illuminated with stars. It had a couple of small stores, pubs, one school, a community centre, and not much else. As a teenager, Robyn couldn't wait to move away from the place. Apart from the fact that there was nothing to do, everyone knew who she was.

Moving to the city meant being able to blend in, no longer being the girl with the dead dad. The city wasn't much bigger, but it was more anonymous. People didn't talk to each other the way they did in the town she grew up in. Neighbours didn't pop in at random or relay everything she got up to back to her mom. But on nights like tonight, driving down the dark windy road toward home, Robyn missed the town. With city lights and built up streets, it was rare she ever got a chance to enjoy the unfiltered sky in all its starlit glory. Sipping tea with her mom in the familiar surroundings had made her realise that in running from the bad memories, she had run so far from the good ones too.

As Robyn exited the car park of her building, something

caught her eye. There, on the stairs leading up to her apartment, Lexi sat, looking lost in her thoughts. Robyn's heart started to thump in her chest. She wished at that moment that everything could go back to how it had been right before the fire. Except with the addition of her newfound understanding of what she wanted from life.

But it had been days since their happy bubble had popped. Lexi had barely spoken a word to her since yesterday. She was busy with getting her art done, and the easy, fun way they existed together had disappeared, and Robyn had no idea how to get it back. As she walked closer to the door her heart beat frantically. Tonight had been a good night, and the last thing she wanted was to watch Lexi walk away from her. She flashed back to her mother's words and took a deep breath. Time to power through.

Lexi seemed to snap out of the daze she was in as she lifted her eyes to Robyn's. A small, tentative smile graced her lips, and Robyn's heart began to slowly return to its natural rhythm. "I did it."

Robyn stopped, then joined Lexi on the step and smiled in return. "You did?"

Lexi nodded, her eyes taking in Robyn like she'd never seen her before.

"I knew you would," Robyn said.

Lexi tilted her head to the side, an indiscernible look on her face. "You did, didn't you?"

Robyn shrugged, not exactly sure what was happening but preferring it to the distance that had been between them this week.

"You never doubted me," Lexi added softly.

Robyn's forehead creased at the sorrowful tone of Lexi's words. "Why would I?"

Lexi's face crumpled as tears started to cascade down her

face. Robyn instinctively reached out to cup her cheek and felt a rush as Lexi leaned into her touch.

"I'm sorry, Robs."

She dropped her hand as Lexi turned more fully toward her and ran a thumb across Lexi's upturned palm. "For what, Sunny? What happened?"

"I doubted you. The other day I went for lunch with Sam, at Blaze. I bumped into Freya. She asked about the apartment and said she was with you that night and I just…" Lexi trailed off, shame apparent on her features.

Robyn nodded, understanding what Lexi's assumption had been. Indignation rose in her chest, but just as quickly dissipated.

"I didn't sleep with her," Robyn said. Her voice was calm and even, a contrast to Lexi's broken words.

"I know. It was a misunderstanding. But I shouldn't have assumed. I should have just asked you yesterday instead of switching off like I did."

"You should have. But you're also not perfect, which is slightly refreshing. It doesn't feel good that you'd think I would do that after what happened between us. But you acted a little shitty for a day, and then you immediately apologised when you learned the truth. It's kind of annoying, actually."

Lexi's mouth turned up in a small smile as she swiped at her eyes. "Annoying?"

"Yeah. You're weird with all this honest, open communication stuff. It's hard to be broody and mysterious when you're around."

Lexi slid a hand into Robyn's and shivered at the chill picking up in the air. "I promise to try my best to give you plenty of brooding opportunities in the future."

Robyn laughed, still running her thumb back and forth over Lexi's hand before mumbling, "Sunny?"

Lexi's smile widened at the moniker as she replied, "Yeah?"

Robyn took a moment to look up at the sky, then lowered her gaze back to Lexi. "What the hell are we doing out here?"

Lexi chuckled and followed Robyn's gaze up to the stars above.

"I was trying to figure out what to say before going up. I thought you'd be back already, so I wanted to have my thoughts gathered. You showed up in the middle of the thought-gathering process. It's pretty, though, isn't it?"

Robyn nodded as Lexi laid her head on Robyn's shoulder. "It reminds me of the time I went camping with my dad. And by camping, I mean he put up a tent in our back garden."

Robyn's shoulder vibrated lightly with Lexi's chuckle.

"Ah yes, back garden camping. I've heard of it. Was it fun?"

Robyn smiled at the memory, allowing space for all the little details to come back to her. "My sisters and I were so excited. My mom stayed indoors because, in her words, *I have a perfectly good bed and plan to use it.*"

She mimicked her mother's voice and Lexi laughed, lifting her head to look at Robyn.

"April and Ava barely lasted an hour before the novelty wore off. It was too cold, and of course the TV was inside. But it was rare I got one-on-one time with my dad, so there was no way I was passing up the opportunity. Even if my lips were turning blue."

Lexi traced a finger across Robyn's bottom lip before stroking her cheek lightly.

"You're almost getting there now. But I want to hear the rest of the story before we head up. Did you tell ghost stories?"

"We did, but they were more silly than scary. When it got really dark, we pulled our sleeping bags out and lay in the grass to look up at the stars. I still remember the feeling I got. I didn't have words for it then. It wasn't a big feeling, not like excitement or anticipation. But now I know I was content. Just me, my dad, and the stars in the sky."

Robyn lowered her gaze to Lexi and placed a soft kiss on her lips as Lexi melted into her touch. She pulled back and tilted her head. "Magic."

Lexi had a dreamy look on her face as she replied, "Magic?"

Robyn nodded, neither of them taking their eyes off the other. "I woke the next morning in my bed. He totally denied carrying me there." Robyn recalled confronting him at the breakfast table the next table, a sparkle in his eye. "He kept saying it wasn't him, must be magic. I was well past the age of believing in that stuff, but it felt magical regardless. Kind of like tonight. Magic."

"I love that," Lexi replied as she leaned closer on the step. Robyn moved her lips to Lexi's ear and whispered softly.

"Now, if I close my eyes, will you teleport us to our apartment before we freeze out here?"

✛

Lexi laughed as they got up to move, keeping their fingers entwined all the while.

"We could just use these magical things we have called legs, Robbie. And you can tell me about your dinner."

Robyn grumbled about the walking part and then began to tell Lexi about her dinner and the conversations with her mom.

"Wow, that's great, Robbie. I'm glad you said all of that. I'm proud of you."

Robyn's cheeks pinked at Lexi's praise as they walked into the apartment.

"Me too. I wish I would've done it sooner," Robyn said.

Lexi tugged at Robyn's hand until she turned so they were face to face. "You did it when you could, and that is enough. You are enough. Don't take away from that by wishing for things you can't change."

Robyn dipped her eyes to Lexi's lips. Lexi paused and then she traced a hand up Robyn's arm slowly.

"You really make me feel like it, you know that?" Robyn whispered.

"Make you feel like what?"

The weight of Robyn's stare made Lexi feel so vulnerable, yet so very safe.

"Enough. You make me feel like I am enough," Robyn said.

Lexi reached up and pressed her lips to Robyn's, unable to hold back any longer. She wrapped her arms around Robyn's neck and kissed her, pouring everything into the action.

"You are. Truly."

They kissed for a long time, getting lost in each other, their arms staying firmly wrapped around each other. Neither of them moved to take it further, no wandering hands or legs pressed too close. It wasn't the same lust-fuelled embrace as before, but it was so much more. It was soft, gentle, all-consuming, and beautiful, and it made Lexi's heart feel like it was overflowing.

When they finally pulled back, they stared at each other for a long moment. Robyn spoke first. "We can't do anything else until we talk about this. I don't want a repeat of this week. Well, I definitely want to repeat some of it, but you know what I mean."

Lexi smiled and nodded, her lips still numb and tingly. She agreed wholeheartedly in theory. This wasn't just sex. It wasn't just passion. They deserved to make sure it was treated with care. But Robyn was just too damn good at kissing. She pressed their lips together again, wanting to savour the moment.

"Lex, this isn't talking." Robyn said the words with a smile, clearly not unhappy with Lexi's persistence. Lexi yawned then, the day catching up with her, along with the lack of sleep from working on her final canvas.

"Tomorrow, we talk. It's late and you need sleep right now," Robyn stated firmly.

The conversation they needed to have would be far too in-depth for this late at night. But the idea of going to bed alone without a resolution was also unappealing. She showed her annoyance with an exaggerated pout, causing Robyn to do that slow shake of her head that always made Lexi grin.

"You're exhausted, Sunny. Sleep."

Lexi moved into Robyn's arms, laid her head on Robyn's chest, and held her tight. Robyn's arms curled around her to keep her close and Lexi wondered if she could sleep right there.

"Come on," Robyn said as she took her hand and walked her toward their bedrooms. As they bypassed Lexi's room and headed straight for Robyn's, her heart fluttered. She wasn't quite sure what was happening, but she had no complaints if it meant being next to Robyn.

"No funny business. Just two people who don't need to be alone right now. Okay?"

Lexi smiled, her heart warming at getting to sleep next to Robyn again. It was weird what you could miss after such a short time. Robyn went to grab pyjamas, while Lexi stripped off her pants and T-shirt and slid under the covers in her matching underwear set.

"Not fair," Robyn said.

Lexi batted her eyelashes innocently. "Hey, I left my underwear on. Too tired to go get pyjamas."

Robyn huffed, grabbing one of her T-shirts to toss to Lexi. "You cannot sleep in underwear tonight, or this sleeping thing won't work out."

Lexi rolled her eyes and grabbed the too large T-shirt and made a show of putting it on before snuggling back up under the covers. "Better?"

Robyn's eyes darkened with lust as she slid in next to her. But she leaned over and placed a chaste kiss on Lexi's mouth before snuggling in behind her.

"Much better."

With Robyn's body pressed against her back, Lexi wondered how she would ever get to sleep. Every inch of her skin tingled with the contact, and she desperately wanted more. Robyn placed a soft kiss on her shoulder and ran her thumb back and forth over Lexi's hand in the soothing gesture she was becoming accustomed to. Part of her wanted to turn and take Robyn in her arms and forgo their earlier agreement of talking first. She had no doubt Robyn wanted her, so why were they holding back?

But despite her body's loud desires, Lexi's eyes began to droop. She let out a contented sigh and relaxed back against Robyn, knowing in her heart there would be plenty of time to follow those desires wherever they would lead. The week had been a whirlwind, but Lexi couldn't imagine a better way to bring it to a close. Before long, soft snores greeted her ears. She stopped fighting the tide pulling her under and allowed herself to be lulled into a deep sleep by the comforting sounds.

CHAPTER NINETEEN

Robyn had never been so thankful for the time she got off between shifts as she was waking up with Lexi in her arms that morning. They must have shifted positions during the night because before her eyes even opened, she noticed she was now sleeping on her back with a weight on her chest. She moved her fingers absentmindedly up and down Lexi's skin, an action she kept up as she blinked her eyes open. With her other arm, she held Lexi tight against her, as if to ensure she was really there.

Robyn had spent so much of her adult life delaying opening her eyes until the person she spent the night with had left, for fear that waking next to anyone would create the intimacy she worked so hard to avoid. Yet here she was again, having spent the night holding Lexi, revelling in waking with her body pressed close. Robyn placed a kiss on the top of Lexi's head and chuckled as Lexi burrowed against her. She had planned to ease out from under Lexi and surprise her with breakfast so they could talk, but with the death grip Lexi placed on her at the hint of movement, that was out of the question.

"You awake, Sunny?"

"No." The grumbled, sleepy reply had Robyn laughing. She placed a hand under Lexi's chin and tilted her head up to look at her firmly closed eyelids.

"Oh, okay, sorry. I just wanted a kiss, but that wouldn't be good if you were sleeping. Consent is important."

Lexi's eyelids flew open, and she blinked them innocently. "It is. Important, and sexy."

The small teasing smile that formed on Lexi's lips affected Robyn in more ways than one.

"Sexy, eh?" Robyn asked.

Lexi nodded, shifting so she was lying next to Robyn's face, still half covering her body.

Robyn leaned down, stopping a hair's breadth from Lexi's mouth, close enough that Lexi would feel the whispered words. "Can I please kiss you?"

Lexi's body melted into hers and their lips pressed together in a way Robyn was sure she would never get sick of. She pulled Lexi on top, staggering their legs and deepening the kiss. The T-shirt Lexi wore, Robyn's T-shirt, rode up until Robyn's thigh was pressed against the soft cotton panties beneath. The heat radiating from Lexi's core mirrored her own, and Robyn ached to have every inch of her exposed.

"Robbie. This isn't talking."

Robyn's breathing was laboured, but she couldn't help laughing at Lexi mirroring her own words from the night before. It's like they took it in turns to be the voice of reason, a perfect balance. She traced her fingers in a slow, deliberate path up and down Lexi's spine as they stared at one another, loving the effect playing out on Lexi's face.

"So, let's talk."

Lexi raised both eyebrows, then bit her bottom lip as Robyn pressed against the soft, sensitive spots along her back. "Shouldn't we get dressed first?"

Robyn moved her other arm around Lexi, massaging softly with both hands, pressing Lexi against her thigh with each movement. "I am fully dressed. And you are dressed. In my T-shirt. Which looks hot on you, by the way."

Lexi rolled her eyes and bit back a groan. If the dampness against Robyn's skin was anything to go by, Lexi was getting close.

"I'm not sure this is the optimum setting for a rational conversation," Lexi said.

The tone of Lexi's voice was as much of a turn-on as the body pressed against her. Robyn had to use all of her resolve to maintain her composure and keep her actions slow and steady.

"Do you want me?" Robyn asked.

"Fuck, yes. Isn't that obvious?"

It was, but Robyn still loved to hear it. "Do you want me to stop?"

The tightened grip Lexi placed on her shoulders was enough of an indicator, and Lexi shook her head for good measure. Robyn was more turned on than she had been in her whole life, and she was still fully clothed. She stopped her movements, and the little whine from Lexi sent a tingling through her whole body.

"We're supposed to be talking, remember? You need to say it."

A flash of defiance shot behind Lexi's eyes and Robyn stopped breathing for a moment, utterly transfixed by the image above her.

"No. Don't stop. Please." The last word ended on a whimper which was very nearly Robyn's undoing.

"We both know this is going to happen. There's no conversation that will change the fact that I'm going to watch you fall apart beneath me, slowly but so very surely. So, if you want me to stop at any time, I stop. If not, well, nothing is preventing us from multitasking. You talk, I touch."

Robyn ended the sentence by adding pressure to Lexi's back and pressing her thigh more firmly against her aching centre. Lexi rocked against her and Robyn moved a hand to her ass, halting her movements.

"You're not keeping up your end. You talk, remember?"

Lexi nodded reluctantly and Robyn smiled, making slow, deliberate strokes with her thigh that would drive Lexi to the edge, but not quite over it yet.

"I had all these things I wanted to say, but surprisingly they're escaping me."

Robyn was sure there was nothing in the world sexier than Lexi's husky, lustful tone.

"Why did you doubt me?" Robyn asked.

Surprise flashed through Lexi's eyes that were filled with desire. It clearly wasn't the topic she was expecting.

"Because I've seen Freya."

Robyn shook her head and moved a hand up to cup Lexi's face gently. "You've also seen you. And more importantly, I know you've seen how I look at you. So, I don't buy that answer for a second, Sunny. Where'd the honesty go, hmm?"

Lexi turned her head to place a kiss on Robyn's palm, her face a picture of vulnerability.

"Remember, you're in control here. We can stop and go talk outside," Robyn said.

Lexi shook her head vehemently, taking Robyn's hand from her cheek and moving it behind her. "Don't stop."

The words were clear and unwavering, so Robyn continued her exploration of Lexi's body as Lexi continued talking.

"Robyn, I know you. I know how hard it is for you to trust anyone, to rely on anyone, or let people take care of you."

Robyn had known that Lexi noticed things in ways nobody else did, but hearing how much she truly understood her was a little unnerving.

"You are so damn terrified of being hurt or let down and I let you down I did something really dangerous, and you were mad at me. I get it, I do. I showed you that I was unreliable. I'm working through that, and I am putting things in place to make sure it doesn't happen again, but I wouldn't blame you for not trusting that yet."

Robyn's hands had stopped wandering and they both lay still, staring at each other. Lexi's face was a mixture of want and apprehension. Robyn shook her head slowly before gripping Lexi and switching their positions. She stroked a hand softly down Lexi's face as she adjusted on top of her, pressing a thigh back against the apex of her legs.

"My turn to talk."

Robyn placed a gentle kiss on Lexi's lips, unable to resist. She was so beautiful. Robyn ran her lips along Lexi's jawline and nipped at her earlobe, sucking softly.

"You know a lot about me, you're right. But you were wrong about one thing."

She pulled back and moved her thigh more purposefully now, picking up the pace as Lexi gripped her hips and her breathing got heavier.

"I—what?" Lexi's jumbled words made Robyn feel in control, and it was a feeling she loved. Especially when it came to controlling Lexi's pleasure.

"I wasn't afraid of being let down," Robyn said.

Lexi's eyes fluttered closed as her soft moans began to get more frequent with the friction of their thrusts.

"Eyes open, baby. Look at me."

A thrill shot through her as Lexi obeyed, those beautiful, honey brown eyes landing on hers. She couldn't resist any longer. Lexi falling apart in her arms was becoming a need more than a want. Robyn dropped her hand between them to move the thin cotton fabric to the side, exposing Lexi's swollen clit to her touch. She pressed against it as Lexi's eyes went wide, more than ready for her release.

"I was terrified of loving someone so much that losing them would break me. And when I thought you were in that apartment, in that fire, hurt or scared…Lex, I was broken."

Silent screams emanated from Lexi's mouth and her legs shook as she clenched her thighs around Robyn's hand in the most beautiful display of pleasure Robyn had ever seen.

❖

As Lexi's brain started to return to her body, after what could only be described as a mind-blowing orgasm, she replayed Robyn's words in her head. *Wait, was she saying what it sounded like she was saying?* Lexi blinked her eyes open and stared at Robyn, who was hot as hell hovering above her. She should probably be subtle about it in case she misunderstood, maybe get Robyn to repeat herself or clarify the meaning, but her mouth had other ideas.

"You're saying you love me."

Subtlety had never been her strong suit. Robyn smiled tentatively, and the self-assured confidence that had been radiating from her all morning made way for a flash of uncertainty.

"I guess I am?" Robyn spoke it as a question, and Lexi couldn't help the smile it produced. The fact that she was smiling gave Robyn back the confidence she needed to remove any hint of questioning from her words.

"I am. I know it's way too soon to say that. We haven't even had an actual date yet, so all of this is like the definition of jumping the gun. But I don't know how to explain it without just saying it."

Robyn moved to lie beside Lexi, and they both turned

to face one another. Lexi slid a hand into Robyn's, already missing the skin to skin contact she was becoming accustomed to.

"You brought me to a car boot sale. That's a top tier date," Lexi said.

Robyn shook her head, a small smile tugging at the corner of her mouth. "Firstly, you're weird. Secondly, we weren't even dating then."

"I beg to differ. You surprised me with something I loved. You carried my bags. I bought you lunch and invited myself to your sister's anniversary party. That all sounds like date territory to me. Speaking of which, the party was our second date. And since I am a low-key kinda girl, our day together here was definitely date number three. We're basically in a long-term relationship at this point."

Robyn's laughter would need to be added to the list of sounds she made that Lexi loved. She ran a finger up and down Robyn's arm slowly, wanting to hear more from that list sooner rather than later.

"So, we've basically just fast-forwarded past the wooing stage of our romance? Sounds like a cop-out to me."

Lexi shook her head slowly, moving to palm Robyn's breast and relishing the sight of Robyn's widening eyes locked on hers. "Oh, no. There will be plenty of wooing. But let's not pretend we haven't been more than just friends since before we let our bodies show it."

She dipped her head to pull a hardened nipple into her mouth, sucking and licking as Robyn ran a hand through her hair to pull her closer. She took it in turns to lavish attention on one and then the other of Robyn's breasts. She had never known she could be as addicted to someone's body as she found herself with Robyn's. Nothing sounded better than spending hours getting lost in every inch, every curve. She wanted to make a map of each spot that made Robyn sigh or moan or shiver and revisit them often.

"Lexi, what are you doing to me?"

She moved her lips slowly up to Robyn's, pressing her back against the mattress and kissing her slowly. With their lips still brushing against one another, she whispered softly.

"Loving me might be scary, Robs. It might even break you sometimes. But I will always put you back together again."

Before Robyn could utter a word, Lexi turned, suddenly wanting nothing more than for them to get lost in each other together. She straddled Robyn's chest and ran a tongue slowly down her body until she reached her destination. A thrill shot through her at the muffled expletives Robyn uttered as she wound her arms around Lexi's thighs and pulled Lexi back toward her eager mouth.

The sensation of Robyn's lips and tongue moving over every inch of her hot, sensitive core spurred Lexi on. She used her hands to part Robyn's thighs, and then to expose the flesh that glistened for her. She ran her tongue up and down across the surface in leisurely strokes. As Robyn picked up the pace, Lexi had no choice but to follow, lost in the building sensations between her own legs. They moved in tandem, creating a perfect rhythm without exchanging a single word.

Lexi's brain was filled with Robyn. The taste of Robyn on her tongue. The scent of passion permeating the air around them. The feel of Robyn's lips against her. The sight of Robyn, vulnerable and wanting, beneath her. The sounds she elicited with every shifting stroke. Lexi's senses were truly, completely overwhelmed by Robyn.

She wrapped her lips around Robyn's swollen nub as Robyn mimicked her actions. Stars formed behind her eyes and her knees gave out as Robyn held her tight. She didn't want to stop riding this sea of pleasure together, but her body couldn't hold out any longer. As Robyn's thighs clenched around her, ripples moved through her own, and they both exploded with melodious moans.

She took a moment to catch her breath, her head resting against Robyn's thigh as she traced circles with her fingers along the other one.

"Wow." The utterance from Robyn made her laugh because of the sheer understatement of the word. Wow indeed. Lexi willed her body to work, but it didn't feel like moving.

"I want to lie next to you, but my body refuses to move."

Robyn's body shook as she chuckled against her leg. Then with a shuffle, Robyn manoeuvred herself out from under Lexi and joined her at the end of the bed.

"Better?" Robyn asked.

"Mmm. My hero."

Robyn rolled her eyes at Lexi's sleepy statement, but Lexi stood her ground.

"You are, though." She kept her eyes trained on Robyn's, ensuring the sincerity in her words was clear. Robyn's face softened in a smile, her eyes glistening in a way she would likely never admit to after the fact.

"Oh, just in case it wasn't clear, I love you too," Lexi said.

CHAPTER TWENTY

I was afraid too, you know."

The words came so out of the blue that it took Robyn a moment to place them. They had eventually vacated the bedroom in search of food and had found a new psychological thriller to watch while eating. Lexi sat between her legs with her back against Robyn on their couch, their empty plates strewn along the table in front of them. The end credits to the movie had filled the screen, but Robyn knew Lexi's fear wasn't in relation to that.

"Afraid of what, Sunny?"

"This. Us. Losing you. I don't just mean romantically. Yes, it's amazing, but I was more afraid of losing you from my life. We've been roommates, and friends, for far longer, and I love that. Falling in love with you is a little surreal, but loving you isn't something new to me, you know? Losing you would've hurt like hell regardless of that."

Robyn processed the words and their sincerity. It was true, of course. If the fire had happened weeks ago, before they ventured down this path, would she have worried any less about Lexi? Would she have cared any less if something happened? By that logic, her fear of their growing relationship was losing its grip.

"And let's be real here. I paint pictures in the relative

safety of my studio or our apartment, assuming I steer clear of the cooker, that is. You run into burning buildings for a living. I think if anyone has the right to panic about winding up broken, it's me."

Robyn scooched back and Lexi turned to face her.

"I know my job can be dangerous. I can promise you I take it very seriously, and I don't take unnecessary risks. I will always do what I can to keep myself safe and stop that from happening."

Lexi nodded at Robyn's words and squeezed her hand, but kept silent, giving Robyn time to continue.

"But I can't pretend it's not a valid fear. I'm living proof of it. But I am a firefighter. I love what I do, and that's unlikely to change."

Robyn's heart thumped wildly as she watched Lexi's face, hoping to catch a glimpse of her thoughts. "Your opinion matters to me, more than even I knew. Being a firefighter was my whole life, up until now. Until you."

Sure, Robyn had family and friends she loved, but ultimately, her job took precedence over everything. That would change for Lexi. She didn't plan to jump into something serious with Lexi and expect her to take a constant back seat to work.

"My career will always be important to me. But this"— she gestured between them—"will be too. My life with you is already more important than I ever imagined, and I know that's only going to grow."

Tears filled Lexi's eyes, but the small smile that appeared on her lips gave Robyn the comfort to continue.

"I want to make sure those things are compatible. It's a lot to ask of you, to be okay with the person you are building a life with putting themselves in harm's way on a regular basis.

I understand someone being unwilling to sign up for that. But that's what I want, Lexi. To build a life with you."

She paused and took a breath, hoping the tears that were now overflowing down Lexi's cheeks were good tears.

"I told you yesterday, Robyn. I know you."

Lexi pulled both of Robyn's hands into her lap, tilting her head before she continued speaking. "I see how much your work means to you. I would never ask you to give that up. My father spent a long time trying to convince me to stop painting. I know it's not the same thing, it's not the same kind of risk. The biggest risk for me is never having financial security, or safety, or a damn pension plan."

Lexi laughed at that, but her eyes showed how fresh the wounds were. "I mean, he was right. Look at what happened even recently with my creative block. I have raw talent, I know that. But I haven't gotten to where I am based purely on that. I also have connections, and an awesome understanding roommate who doesn't yell at me for the paint splatters."

"Often," Robyn replied, quickly pointing to a few new ones that adorned the side of their television stand.

Lexi grimaced and shrugged, her smile returning. "The kind of career I want isn't financially safe, but I couldn't walk away from it. It's an integral part of who I am."

Robyn nodded, understanding completely. "Our paths and passions are so vastly different, but our experiences are surprisingly similar."

Lexi linked their fingers together and pulled their hands up to her mouth, placing a soft kiss on the back of Robyn's.

"You're a firefighter. I'm an artist. I don't expect that to change, and I don't want it to. I'm sure it won't be this simple with everything, and we will have plenty more to figure out. But I don't doubt that we can. Because it just feels right, doesn't it? This all feels so right. And I've learned that those feelings are rarely wrong."

Robyn wasn't one to follow her feelings often. She spent so long suppressing them that she didn't know if she could. She followed rules, logic, orders, but feelings? Not so much. Except she agreed with everything Lexi said. It *did* feel right. They would have so much more to work through, especially considering they were entering a new relationship while already living together. But none of that worried her because it would fall into place, one day at a time.

"I feel like a pod person. What are you doing to me?" Robyn said with a frown.

Lexi giggled and leaned in to kiss her softly. "Am I going to have to work harder to unleash grumpy Robyn in future? That could be a deal breaker for me."

Robyn's frown turned to a scowl as she crossed her arms indignantly.

"Never mind, we're good," Lexi said, then shrieked as Robyn found the ticklish spot behind her knee.

"I surrender," Lexi yelled between laughs.

Robyn moved her hand to the side and slowly up her thigh as she asked, "You sure?"

Lexi's breath hitched and she nodded as Robyn kissed her softly. They had spent the morning exploring every inch of each other, and Robyn was more than ready to do it all over again. Lexi's face was like an open book, showing Robyn exactly what she liked. She would never get sick of Lexi's many and varied expressions. Robyn wanted to spend the rest of her life memorising each and every one.

"I surrender too, Sunny."

❖

"It's just been perfect. I know that's a cliché, but it has."

Lexi was sporting a cheesy smile, but she couldn't help it. It had been a week since she and Robyn had finally been honest about their feelings, and life was better than she could have imagined. A fact which she was gleefully sharing with Sam and Brooke over dinner at their house, with Robyn by her side. Their first double date.

"Look how smitten you are. It's adorable." Brooke fanned her eyes and Sam laughed at the display. "Ugh, these hormones are no joke. I'm just so happy for you."

Lexi found herself getting choked up in response, without the pregnancy hormones to blame. She was so grateful for them both, for everything that led her to them and to a place where she was surrounded by support.

"Okay, you two. Stop with the emotions. We're celebrating, remember?"

Sam was right. They were celebrating more than her love life. She glanced over at Robyn, whose face already held a hint of pink at the attention.

"You didn't need to go to all this effort. But this food is amazing." Robyn pointed to her plate with her fork to emphasize her point.

"Of course we did. A promotion is a big deal. And I figured the last time I tried to make you something special in the culinary department didn't end too well, so I enlisted help." Lexi laughed as Robyn shook her head, an amused expression on her face.

"Oh, we're joking about that now? That's a positive. And yes, I was glad to help," Sam said, as she got a playful scoff from Brooke.

"Help? You played video games with our son while I cooked every bit of this meal."

Sam shrugged nonchalantly. "I entertained the kid. That's helping. Plus, I made the gravy."

Lexi laughed at the back and forth, knowing full well it was more likely Finley entertained Sam rather than the other way around. Clearly, lacking skills in the kitchen ran in the family too.

"Oh, did I tell you about the cooker?" Lexi interjected, the conversation bringing it to mind. "You know I've been really worried since the fire and trying to make sure it doesn't happen again."

Robyn's hand covered hers and squeezed gently as Lexi continued.

"Robyn went and bought this thing I didn't even know existed, a stove monitor. It gives a notification if you forget to turn off the stove and can sound an alarm. I know that's totally not romantic and shouldn't make me fall even more in love with her, but it totally does."

She glanced over to where Robyn was looking at her even more lovingly, and gratitude filled her all over again.

"Adding that to my list of things to get," Sam laughed, "but I get it, that's pretty awesome. It shows Robyn is trying to help you, not just expecting you to do something you struggle with, like remember. That earns you major points."

Sam directed the last sentence to Robyn, who tried to shrug it off but had a wide smile across her face.

Lexi nodded animatedly. "That's exactly it. And when I began thinking back on it, I realised Robyn has been doing things like that for years."

The hand in hers squeezed tighter and Lexi turned her attention to Robyn. "You have. You bought that tracker thing for my keys when I kept losing them last year. You make me food and just put it in front of me when I get lost in a painting.

You put that whiteboard on the wall, where I write things I know I'll forget to tell you."

"You're making me swoon," she heard Sam say, and saw her fanning herself out of the corner of her eye. But Lexi's gaze was locked on Robyn's face. Unashamedly bragging about Robyn was going to be a new hobby of hers.

"You've been helping me long before we kissed. Daily life with you is the part I'm most excited about. The mind-blowing sex has just been an added bonus."

Robyn's face went red, but her eyes darkened with a look Lexi knew well. One that meant they'd barely make it back to the apartment before her clothes came off.

"Okay, now you're just showing off," Sam joked. "I'm really happy for you both. Some people appreciate flowers and chocolates, but everything you just listed there is a lot more thoughtful in my eyes. It's obvious to anyone with eyes how perfect you fit."

Robyn's phone rang and she excused herself to take the call. Lexi knew it likely meant their lust-fuelled rendezvous would have to wait. A promotion meant more responsibility, including last minute calls to the station.

"Sorry, guys. Duty calls. This has all been amazing, though. Thank you."

Robyn confirmed Lexi's thoughts and grabbed her coat, leaning in to kiss her softly. "I might be late, so don't wait up, but I'll see you at home as soon as I can."

Lexi's heart filled at the words *I'll see you at home*, as Robyn said her goodbyes.

"Go be a hero, Moore," Sam said, and Lexi smiled. That's exactly what Robyn was.

Lexi went home that night and glanced at her bed, the one she hadn't slept in all week. She changed into the T-shirt

Robyn had given her that she had now claimed as her own and walked to Robyn's room, hesitating a moment. It would be the first night she would be going to bed alone since they'd discussed their feelings. Would Robyn expect to come home to an empty bed? Would she want to?

Although she was sure about Robyn, maybe they should have a talk about their sleeping situation before she made any more assumptions. She went back to her own room and crawled under the covers, falling quickly into a dreamless sleep.

When she awoke in the early hours of the morning, it was to the feel of a strong arm wrapped around her from behind and a warm body pressed against her back. She was safe and secure, wrapped up in Robyn's embrace, and a sense of calm washed over her. Whether they slept in her bed or Robyn's, it didn't matter. She was exactly where she belonged. *Home.*

Epilogue

"Wake up, sleepyhead!"

Robyn woke to Lexi bouncing on her bed and groaned, pulling the pillow up over her face. It had been six months since they had become a couple, and they'd fallen into a good rhythm. They had breakfast together most mornings and fell asleep together most nights, unless Robyn was on shift. The nights she worked, she would usually find Lexi in her bed after and crawl in beside her, falling asleep quicker than she ever managed before. Particularly on difficult shifts.

The days she didn't work, they spent time together, either alone or with their friends or family. Lexi had been a big part of the better, stronger relationship Robyn began to build with her mother, and the rest of Robyn's family thought Lexi was the best thing to ever happen to her. So, in April's words, they were around more to make sure she didn't screw it up.

Lexi had spent the previous night at Sam and Brooke's, babysitting while they had a night out, and was now apparently back and on a mission.

"How about you come snuggle in here, instead?" Robyn poked her head out from under the pillow, hoping to entice Lexi into joining her and avoiding the morning a little longer.

"Not gonna happen. If I get in there, we won't leave for

at least an hour, and that doesn't work with my plans," Lexi replied.

Robyn attempted a pout, but that was more Lexi's area of expertise. She knew how to aim those at exactly the right time to melt any and all of Robyn's resolve.

"But I'm sleepy and I want to kiss you, Sunny."

Lexi hopped off the bed and leaned a hip against the door frame, grinning. "You can. Over here."

She tapped her lips for good measure and Robyn huffed.

"Not fair. Why do I have to get up so early? What's your grand plan that's better than joining me in bed to get far more kisses?"

Lexi crossed her arms to indicate she wasn't budging. "It's ten a.m., not early. I waited as long as I could before waking you. And it's a surprise. You can make up for those kisses later, I promise."

Lexi's salacious tone sent a thrill through Robyn, something she was still getting used to. Every day, she wondered if Lexi's effect on her would even out. Not fade exactly, but become expected. And every day she was surprised at its continued intensity. She pulled back the covers and got out of bed, going to claim her kiss.

Lexi made the kiss a worthy prize but made sure they didn't get too carried away, clearly on a schedule. Early morning wake-ups, before the more recent fun reasons, usually meant car boot sales requiring Robyn's car. Lexi had gotten insured under her car recently so that she could borrow it whenever Robyn didn't need it, something Robyn insisted upon. But Lexi might just want company, a thought that didn't make her grumble as much as it would have before. Wandering around stalls, watching Lexi's eyes light up at some seemingly benign object was now an appealing prospect.

She got dressed under Lexi's orders and met her at the door. She wore tight black jeans and a white shirt with the top buttons open, unsure of what the outing would call for so aiming for smart casual. The look on Lexi's face said she made the right choice.

"My eyes are up here, Sunny."

"Good thing I was looking at your boobs then, baby." Lexi winked at Robyn and laughed at the pink adorning her cheeks. She was too good at ruffling Robyn's feathers, and she knew it.

Lexi insisted on driving, wanting to keep the location a secret. As they got to the car and began the journey, Robyn tried to figure out which location the car boot sale was at. Confusion hit as they headed to the other side of the city centre. Lexi parked along the street and Robyn frowned before she followed Lexi's gaze to a brick building in the corner, which she vaguely recognized as an art gallery.

Maybe this was why Lexi didn't want to say anything, because the last time she subjected Robyn to an exhibition of abstract art pieces, Robyn had grumbled about not understanding what any of it was supposed to be. They did in fact walk to the gallery which appeared to be empty, apart from a woman in a side office who waved to Lexi as they entered. Lexi's hand shook slightly in hers and Robyn halted their movements, turning Lexi to face her.

"What are we doing here?"

Lexi took a deep breath, then smiled tentatively and walked backward, waving her hands toward the walls of the open space. "You're getting a sneak preview of my exhibition."

Robyn shook her head, sure she misheard. "*Your* exhibition? How am I only hearing about this now?"

She turned her head to the side, and the first piece that

caught her eye was the canvas Lexi had transformed from an angry X that day in their apartment, now hanging on a white wall in full display. It still took Robyn's breath away.

"I wanted to surprise you. I started with that first piece over there, which you already know about. I spoke to Muriel, who runs this gallery, about my ideas, and she offered me space to showcase. Starting with this exhibition, but all going well, I'll have a permanent spot here."

Robyn pulled Lexi in and crushed her in a tight hug, overcome with pride. Lexi laughed, hugging her back before releasing her with a soft, "Go look first!"

Needing no more prompting, she walked past the first canvas and took in the rest, emotions crashing through her body with each piece. Although the paintings weren't clear images, Robyn understood every one of them.

"It's our story."

Lexi nodded, linking her fingers with Robyn's. "That's mainly why I wanted to show you first. I had planned to surprise you at the exhibition opening night, but I realised that this is personal to you too. Most people won't understand the depth of the stories behind each canvas, but you do, and I wanted to know if you're okay with it being up here on display. The good, and the bad."

Robyn saw the orange and black swirls, two faces separated by the dark smoke between. A clear depiction of the fire that almost drove a wedge between them. Then beside it, a painting done in mostly varying shades of green, except the outline of black heeled shoes. It took Robyn a moment to place it. Green for jealousy—the heels for the catalyst of Lexi's jealousy. Robyn would never fathom how Lexi's brain came up with these concepts.

The next one had Robyn stopping in her tracks. It already had a Reserved sticker over the title sign, indicating it wasn't for sale. Most of the canvas was a dark sky, dotted with thousands of stars, along with some swirls coming from what looked like a wand. At the very corner, a tiny image showed the shape of a tent and two figures holding hands. One adult and one child. Robyn and her father.

"How did you…" Robyn choked up, trailing off as Lexi wrapped an arm around her waist.

"When you told me about that memory and how it changed things in your mind, I couldn't get it out of my head. I had to paint it. I've reserved it because it's for you, and I can remove it from the exhibit altogether if you want. I just wanted you to see where it fit in our story."

Robyn shook her head, willing her eyes to stop leaking so she could get her words out. "No, no, it's not okay, Sunny. It's the best thing anyone has ever done for me. I adore it. Don't you dare take it down. Once every one of these amazing pieces is sold, which I have no doubt they will be, we will take it home and put it up on our wall. Until then, it stays here."

Lexi nodded, smiling brightly and placing a soft kiss on Robyn's cheek. Robyn continued, marvelling at each piece, and there were so many. Some obvious to her, some she had to ask Lexi to explain, and each one a small part of the story that brought them here today. Clearly Lexi had been very busy while Robyn was on shifts. There were more paintings here than Robyn had ever seen her do before.

The last piece looked like a collage, and as Robyn studied it more closely, that's exactly what it was. It was filled with tiny replicas of each canvas placed together, some overlapping each other, with stitches interwoven between. If you stepped back and looked at the entire image, it looked like two profiles interlocked. She glanced at the title and smiled.

All our broken pieces make us whole.

About the Author

J.J. Hale has been devouring books since she was able to hold one and has dreamt about publishing romance novels with queer leading ladies since she discovered such a thing existed, in her late teens.

The last few years have been filled with embracing and understanding her neurodiversity, which has expanded the dream to include representing kick-ass queer, neurodivergent women who find their happily ever afters.

Jess lives in the south of Ireland, and when she's not daydreaming, she works in technology, plays with LEGO, and (according to the kids) fixes things.

Website: www.jjhaleauthor.com
Email: jjhaleauthor@gmail.com
Twitter: @OverthinkerJess
Facebook & Instagram: @jjhaleauthor

Books Available From Bold Strokes Books

A Degree to Die For by Karis Walsh. A murder at the University of Washington's Classics Department brings Professor Antigone Weston and Sergeant Adriana Kent together—first as opposing forces and then as allies as they fight together to protect their campus from a killer. (978-1-63679-365-8)

Finders Keepers by Radclyffe. Roman Ashcroft's past, it seems, is not so easily forgotten when fate brings her and Tally Dewilde together—along with an attraction neither welcomes. (978-1-63679-428-0)

Homeland by Kristin Keppler and Allisa Bahney. Dani and Kate have finally found themselves on the same side of the war, but a new threat from the inside jeopardizes the future of the wasteland. (978-1-63679-405-1)

Just One Dance by Jenny Frame. Will Taylor Spark and her new business to make dating special—the Regency Romance Club—bring sparkle back to Jaq Bailey's lonely world? (978-1-63679-457-0)

On My Way There by Jaycie Morrison. As Max traverses the open road, her journey of impossible love, loss, and courage mirrors her voyage of self-discovery leading to the ultimate question: If she can't have the woman of her dreams, will the woman of real life be enough? (978-1-63679-392-4)

A Talent Within by Suzanne Lenoir. Evelyne, born into nobility, and Annika, a peasant girl with a deadly secret, struggle to change their destinies in Valmora, a medieval world controlled by religion, magic, and men. (978-1-63679-423-5)

Transitioning Home by Heather K O'Malley. An injured soldier realizes they need to transition to really heal. (978-1-63679-424-2)

Truly Enough by J.J. Hale. Chasing the spark of creativity may ignite a burning romance or send a friendship up in flames. (978-1-63679-442-6)

Vintage and Vogue by Kelly and Tana Fireside. When tech whiz Sena Abrigo marches into small-town Owen Station, she turns librarian Hazel Butler's life upside down in the most wonderful of ways, setting off an explosive series of events, threatening their chance at love…and their very lives. (978-1-63679-448-8)

The Accidental Bride by Jane Walsh. Spinsters Miss Grace Linfield and Miss Thea Martin travel to Gretna Green to prevent a wedding, only to discover a scandalous passion—for each other. (978-1-63679-345-0)

Broken Fences by Jo Hemmingwood. Former army sergeant Seneca Twist has difficulty adjusting to civilian life until she meets psychologist Robyn Mason and has a place to call home. (978-1-63679-414-3)

Never Kiss a Cowgirl by Ali Vali. Asher Evans dreams of winning the National Finals Rodeo in Vegas, and Reagan Wilson wants no part of something that brings back the memory of what killed her father. (978-1-63679-106-7)

Pantheon Girls by Jean Copeland. Cassie Burke never anticipated the detour life is about to take when a meeting with a prospective client reunites her with a past love and reignites the star-crossed passion they shared twenty years earlier. (978-1-63679-337-5)

Roux for Two by Aurora Rey. For TV chef Chelsea Boudreaux and hometown boy Bryce Cormier, love proves as tricky as making a good pot of gumbo. (978-1-63679-376-4)

Starting Over by Nance Sparks. Jennifer has no idea if she can mend Sam's broken soul after the sudden loss of her wife, but it's never too late for starting over. (978-1-63679-409-9)

Three Wishes by Anne Shade. A magic lamp, a beautiful Jinni, and a cursed princess make for one unbelievable story. (978-1-63679-349-8)

Undiscovered Treasures by MJ Williamz. For Cyl and her friends Luna and Martinique, life's best treasures often appear when they're not looking. (978-1-63679-449-5)